Heart of Stone

Also by Sylvia Holloman

Opening Jerred's Eyes

Heart of Stone

Sylvia Holloman

ASTA
PUBLICATIONS

www.astapublications.com

Heart of Stone
Copyright © Sylvia Holloman, 2008

Library of Congress Cataloging-in Publication Data

Holloman, Sylvia

Heart of Stone/Sylvia Holloman

    p. cm.

Includes index

ISBN: 1-934947-06-7
ISBN 13: 978-1-934947-06-7

LCCN: 2008924310

First Printing Asta Publications trade paperback edition March 2008.
Second Printing Asta Publications trade paperback edition January 2009

1.   African-American- Contemporary Fiction. 2. Romance-Fiction. 3.
Relationships-Fiction. I. Title

Printed in the United States of America.

Dedications

I would like to dedicate this book to my children, and my Uncle, Bill Harrington. To some he was just a man, but to me...a hero!

I would like to say a special 'thank you' to my publisher-ASTA Publications, a publishing house built on honor, pride, and quality work. I am driven by their desire, and the gift God gave them to help others.

Chapter 1

"Linc, can't I persuade you to stay?"

Linc had already slipped his clothing back on, stepped into his shoes, and finished buttoning his leather coat as he made his way out of the bedroom towards the front door. He spoke over his broad shoulder to the young lady. He noticed her tousled hair, and on her face, he found what he knew would be there. Satisfaction!

"No, baby, my work here is done!"

The young woman shrugged her bare shoulders, and placed her nude body back underneath the covers to keep warm.

Linc Stone left the young woman's apartment, knowing that he had successfully tucked her in for the night.

It was very cold out, and the snow was coming down fast. Lincoln sat in his vehicle cuffing his ungloved hands together blowing inside of them trying to aid his body heat to circulate. He was waiting for the automobile to warm up just enough to take off.

While Linc sat, he watched the snowflakes dissolve as they hit the windshield of his SUV. With a sharp eye he tried to count their unique shapes and sizes.

Linc was looking for anything to take his mind off of the last few hours. Hell, if he were truthful with himself, the last twenty years. Funny, Linc was starting to identify his encounters with woman to those snowflakes. How lovely they were in the beginning as they landed, and then just like that, the beauty of it was all gone. But, isn't that the price you pay when you're a playa? Linc found he was shaking his head at what he recognized to be a bizarre assumption. He smiled at the irony of it all.

Linc put his truck into drive and headed for home. He needed to wash away the remnants of his last conquest. As Linc maneuvered his way through the traffic in downtown Indianapolis, he noticed all of the Christmas lights and decorations. Everything looked so festive. There were still several people out, possibly people preparing for a party to bring in the New Year. Linc wondered briefly about some of the men he saw, the smiles on their faces. They were probably men who couldn't wait to get home to see their wives and their children. But not Linc, he didn't want a wife or children.

Linc was forty, in great physical shape, and financially, he was living the life he wanted. But there were times, like tonight, when Lincoln Stone grew a little weary of his lifestyle. Linc was an entrepreneur by trade, but he also specialized in pleasing beautiful women. They always wanted more, but for him, moments later, the thrill was gone.

Linc Stone, at a very young age, decided that committing to one woman would never do. Not after seeing what it had done to his father and even his younger brother. He wasn't easily wooed into bed. No, Linc was, indeed, very picky about his selection of women. But once they persuaded him to enter, he faithfully hit it, and then left, never looking back!

Twenty minutes later, Linc pulled into his spacious yard. He owned quite a few acres of land, but he didn't utilize all of it. There was no pool or basketball court , even though he had more than enough land to place both. Linc built a nice house that had three bedrooms, an office that was also his gym, and on his back deck he had a Jacuzzi that was designed to hold up to six people.

Linc pulled his truck into the two car garage and went into his house. Once inside, he didn't bother checking for messages. It was too late for business calls, and he was done satisfying women for the night. No, not until after he entered a brand new year would he please another. Linc headed for his bathroom to shower and shave. And once he was done, it was off to his friend Nancy Huston's New Years Eve party.

♥

It was two hours before midnight as everyone patiently waited to press forward into a brand new year. Sonja Davis sat in the large conference room where the party was being held. They were inside a lavish hotel, located in downtown South Bend, Indiana. Sonja was looking out onto the dance floor. All the expensive suits and formal gowns caused that feeling of uneasiness to take over once again.

For the past few years, her friend, Nancy Huston, held a New Year's Eve party for her clients and fellow entrepreneurs. Sonja knew she didn't belong there. She was only at the party because of Nancy. The two had been friends for twenty years. She had asked herself more than once during the course of the night what she was doing there.

At the age of eighteen, the two met, when both girls began working for the same department store. But Nancy, at a young age had big dreams. The simple life was not for her. Nancy went to college and obtained the necessary degrees, and now she buys and sells real estate.

In the past, Sonja had been like most women, just looking for one good man to spend the rest of her life with. But after three children and two marriages under her belt, the only thing that got Sonja excited was a hot bath and a good night's sleep. The last thing on Sonja's mind was a man, especially when her first marriage was to a green-eyed, abusive monster who had given her a first class ticket to Hell. These days, Sonja was happy with just raising her children.

This particular time when Nancy breezed into town, she talked her good friend and employee into coming to one of her fancy events. Sonja didn't consider herself a people person, and tonight she had danced and talked with enough people to last her a lifetime.

It felt as if she had been there forever. The candle in the centerpiece had almost burned out, and Sonja was ready to go home. All she wanted was a hot bath, her comforter, king size bed and her soft pillows. Tonight her house was empty. Her nineteen year old daughter, Tiffany, and twenty-one year old son-in-law, Terrell, were keeping

Tiffany's brothers for the weekend.

Nancy was making the rounds, going from table to table handing out small party gifts along with her new business cards. Sonja was glad Nancy had finally stopped pushing her off on her male friends. Nancy's male friends were way out of Sonja's league, and Nancy knew it. Sonja wasn't impressed with all the big talk and frills. Nancy had known Sonja for a long time. Her idea of fun was watching one of her favorite TV shows, but not tonight. Tonight, Sonja Davis was going to relax, and if she had to dance a few dances, talk to a few good looking men, then she would. Nancy had an agenda when it came to Sonja. It was Nancy's intent to make sure her friend had a good time.

Sonja was sitting at the table frequently checking her watch, trying not to make eye contact with anyone. She had decided it was time to find Nancy, but before she began her search, Sonja looked up from the burned out candle to see her friend headed her way. On her arm, Nancy had a handsome young man, who looked to be in his late twenty's. Sonja just knew Nancy was at it again.

"Sonja, honey, I want you to meet Chad Hinsdale. I sold his father some land recently."

The young man stretched out his hand to Sonja; she kindly accepted it.

"It's nice to meet you Chad." Sonja turned to her friend.

"Nancy, I think it's time for me to leave."

"But you haven't danced with Chad yet!"

The young man, who looked to be no more than twenty-five, took thirty-eight year old Sonja by the hand and led her onto the dance floor. Sonja watched as Nancy made her way over to a small group of men. Sonja noticed one of the men watching her. It was Linc Stone. Linc had danced with Sonja earlier in the evening. He had whirled her around the dance floor as he held her oh so close. Their bodies fit perfectly as they danced, It was as if they had done this before, as if being in his arms was where she belonged. Sonja became intoxicated by his alluring cologne. But once the music ended, he couldn't wait to make his hasty exit.

Nancy had told Sonja all about Linc. This brotha was a permanent member of the playas club. Linc Stone was a forty year old playa and more handsome then any one man deserved to be. But, Linc didn't have time for any woman over thirty-five, or with children.

Nancy noticed Linc watching Sonja and Chad. She knew Linc found Sonja attractive, but he was a playa. She knew that just because Linc looked, it didn't mean he would touch.

Linc watched as Chad moved the woman around the dance floor. He could read the young man's thoughts visibly, even from where he was standing. Linc couldn't blame him; he had the same thoughts when he held her in his arms. She seemed to have some sort of power over his body, he didn't like that.

After their dance, Linc made sure to ignore her for the rest of the evening. But he could see that young Chad had other plans. Nancy's voice brought Linc's attention back to the small crowd.

"So, Linc, how's that new building in Chicago working out for you?"

He and Nancy had meet about four or five years ago. A mutual business associate had introduced them. Line was buying up everything he could get his hands on in Indianapolis. Linc had a knack for buying under cost, making a few minor restorations and selling way above property value. These days, Nancy was helping him find other assets that might rouse his curiosity. She was the one who sought out the property in Chicago for him.

"Had some vandals hit it, pushed my workers back a few weeks. Damn kids!"

"Well, when you took away their hang out, you should have expected a rebellion from them."

It wasn't hard for Nancy to believe Linc had actually forgotten what it was like to be a child. It was only because he thought of her as a close friend that Linc shared his horrible childhood with her.

"They're lucky I didn't call the cops on them. Stupid kids never even noticed the surveillance cameras."

In the midst of the conversation, a beautiful woman had successfully found her way by Linc's side. Linc had danced with the young woman earlier, and from that point on, he couldn't get rid of her. He knew she wanted to spend the rest of the evening with him. Linc Stone wasn't going to bring this New Year, or any New Year, in with her or any other woman.

The young woman moved in closer to Linc's strong body as she spoke.

"Linc, darling, they are only children. Didn't you do stupid things when you were a child?"

Linc lifted his glass and finished what little whiskey he had left inside, and without giving her a side glance, he spoke. "Nope..."

Everyone standing around the group burst into laughter when they saw the smirk on Linc's handsome face. Of course he remembered all the silly things he and his brother found to get into, *that's* why he hadn't called the cops.

The song had ended and Sonja was finished. If she had to walk home, she would. After thanking the young man for the dance, she made her way over to her friend, only to find young Chad fast on her heels.

"Nancy, would you mind it if I had your driver take me back to Dowagiac?"

As Nancy prepared to answer, young Chad piped in. "I can take Ms. Davis home for you, Ms. Huston."

Nancy saw her friend stiffen. She knew the last thing Sonja wanted was to end her evening fighting off the advances of a young man.

"I'll take her."

Everyone turned towards the voice. It had been Linc. Sonja looked at the man and then at Nancy.

"Thank you, but I'm sure Nancy won't mind lending me her driver."

Linc produced a charming smile before he spoke. "I'm sure she wouldn't, but I need to be in Kalamazoo tomorrow anyway. It won't hurt me if I'm there a little early."

Sonja waited for Nancy to say something, but she didn't. Nancy knew her friend, and she knew Sonja wanted nothing to do with a man that promised to be a playa for life. Nancy also knew Linc. One look at her children, and he would take off running.

Linc pulled free from the clinging young woman as he spoke to Sonja in a voice that was as lethal as his appearance. "I won't bite; go grab your coat. I will meet you out front."

The young lady began to pout as Linc freed himself. "Linc, I thought we could bring the New Year in together?"

He didn't answer. Instead, he leaned into Nancy and gave her a goodnight kiss on the cheek before saying goodbye to the rest of the bystanders.

Nancy walked Sonja to the coat room to retrieve her coat.

"If I didn't think you were going to be safe, I wouldn't let him drive you."

"I know Nancy, but I have my pepper spray just in case."

The women laughed and hugged before saying their goodbyes.

Sonja stepped outside the hotel just as Linc pulled his green metallic Range Rover Sport up to the curb. He got out of the vehicle, went around and opened the passenger side door. He moved with such superiority. As Sonja got in, Linc leaned over and fastened her seatbelt. His shoulder gently brushed just across her breast, and once again she got a good whiff of his spicy cologne. As he got behind the wheel and fastened his seatbelt, Linc noticed Sonja seemed a little adamant. Linc knew she was a little nervous. He needed her to relax; he didn't want her to be uncomfortable.

"What's your address? I need to program it into my navigational system."

Sonja rattled off her address for him and watched as he programmed it in.

"So, how long have you lived in Dowagiac?"

Sonja didn't look at him, she just spoke, "I was born in Dowagiac."

"Oh, I see. So how long have you and Nancy been friends?"

Sonja gave him a questioning look.

"I'm just trying to make conversation. We are going to be together for almost an hour, just trying to be friendly."

Her demeanor softened slightly. "Nancy and I met when we were eighteen. Once her business took off, she decided her main office would be in Dowagiac. So she purchased a building and hired me to manage it. How did the two of you meet?"

Linc went over briefly how he and Nancy hooked up. And then they were silent for a few moments. Linc was feeling relaxed and at ease; he was glad he had decided to drive her home. He was enjoying the warm feeling he was getting from her, it was a good feeling. He found that he wanted to know everything about her. What she liked, didn't like, what it would take to satisfy her, that sort of thing. He could not deny it; Sonja Davis turned him on. Linc decided to just be blunt.

"So Sonja, what is it you like most about making love? Do you enjoy foreplay? Do you like it fast, or slow?"

Sonja's head whipped around so she could look at his face. Was he serious? No, he couldn't be. He didn't know her like that.

"Why would you need to know something as personal as that?"

Linc took a quick look at her, and then focused on the road again. His voice was still deep and demanding, yet smooth, velvety.

"You are a good looking woman, so it's not unusual for any man to wonder what it would take to please a woman like you."

He gave her another look; it was a quick one, but full of significance.

Damn this man was fine. And that voice could melt the panties off of any woman. Sonja determined that she could look at him and listen to him talk all night. She was sure he had that affect on every woman he came in contact with.

"From what I understand, you don't need to know these things. You just have this way of pleasing women."

"Right, but you seem to be different. And you might require...special treatment. For that, I might need to know a few things. I'm thinking, I wouldn't mind pleasing you."

Sonja gave him another look. Was this man crazy? No, he's just messing with her mind. That's what guys who call themselves "playas" do. Well, maybe she would just give him a taste of his own medicine.

"Umm, I don't know if you're up for the job. I've been married twice, and I have three children. And to tell you the truth, none of the men I've been with has ever pleased me in bed."

Now it was Linc's turn to give her the look of disbelief. She could see the wheels in his mind turning with all sorts of questions.

Sonja smiled at her victory. Just then the system told Linc at the next light he needed to turn right. Her home was the third house on the right.

Linc was silent the rest of the way. His mind was working overtime.

He pulled into Sonja's driveway and went to open the car door for her. Linc walked Sonja to the front door where he used her key to unlock it.

"Thank you for the ride."

Linc wasn't ready to leave her. "Aren't you going to invite me in for some coffee? I still have a long ride ahead of me, and I wouldn't want to fall asleep."

"I'm sorry. Sure, come inside. I will fix us some coffee."

Linc entered and locked her door behind him. He noticed that she took off her shoes, so he removed his, too. He hung both their coats on the rack next to the door and placed his keys on the small polished wooden table that sat against the wall. Sonja headed for the kitchen and Linc followed.

"I have a little cream liquor, would you like a small amount in your coffee to help warm you up?"

"Sure, if you're having some."

Linc took his coat and dinner jacket off and placed them on the back of the chair before sitting down. He never took his eyes off of Sonja as she made her way around her kitchen.

"Are you hungry? I can get us some snack foods?"

"Sure, whatever you have."

"Okay, first I'm going to go change and check my messages. I want to make sure the kids didn't call while I was out."

"I will be right here."

Linc reached inside his jacket pocket, pulled out his cell phone and turned it to vibrate. He knew before long, someone would be calling, and he didn't want to be disturbed.

When Sonja returned, she was wearing a loose-fitting sweat suit and a pair of furry house slippers. She had washed her face; it was make-up free. She was even more beautiful.

She looked at Linc for a moment before she spoke. He had been so frank with her earlier she decided she would do the same with him. She was curious as to why he was forty and still a playa for life. Sonja took a container of dip from the refrigerator before she grabbed a bag of chips and a bowl as she sat across from Linc.

"So, Linc, tell me. What woman broke your heart?"

"What are you talking about? I never said anyone broke my heart."

"No, you didn't have to, your actions, they speak for you. You have very little re-spect for women. And you won't let any woman get too close."

Linc took in her words with great interest. Linc had known this woman for a little over three hours and already she was reading him. What had really blown his mind was… any other woman would have come out of the room butt naked and begging

Linc to put it on her. He was enjoying her company. Linc could tell that Sonja was a very special woman. When the right man bonded with her, he was going to be ex-tremely lucky. Sonja gave off a sense of peace that made one feel like opening up to her was the right thing to do. What the hell? After tonight, he wouldn't be seeing her again. He cautiously told Sonja the tale of his adventure at the game of love.

"My dad met my mom his last year of high school; he fell head over heels for her. She was sixteen and very beautiful, my dad just had to have her. On their third date, she got pregnant with me. So Dad married her and took a job in the factory to sup-port us. My dad never gave her reason to cheat on him, but she did every chance she got. No one could understand her. My father was handsome, and women wanted him."

Sonja listened to him intensely as she nibbled on chips. "So, it was the way your mother treated your father that broke your heart?"

"I learned to keep my guard up. And then I met Connie. Connie was beautiful, just like Mom, and like my dad, I wanted to give her everything. But apparently, she had other plans. One night after she started a fight, she left. Later I found her and some dude all hugged up in the movie theatre."

"That sounds familiar." Sonja shook her head from her own drama.

"You've been there, huh?"

"Yes."

Linc just watched her for a moment as he noticed the pain cross her face while she recalled a bad memory.

"So, after that, I decided I wouldn't give my heart to any woman. Why should I give up my heart when I can have as many women as I want?"

"That's got to get lonely at times?"

"Not really, not when I think of what brought me to this point. What about you? Who broke your heart?"

Sonja told Linc about her first marriage and how it didn't work. She left out the part about her first husband, Josh being a whore, and how he was mentally and verbally abusive. But she had been blessed with her Tiffany, and a few years later, her Matthew. After years of abuse, Sonja had enough. He had embarrassed her, but the mental stress she found on her daughter's Tiffany's face was too much. Her son, Matthew, thank goodness, was too young to fully understand. Sonja snapped out of it and decided she would no longer put her children through that, so she divorced her first husband,Josh. She told him how she met and married Arlando, and along came her third child, Jeffrey . Arlando worked hard, perhaps too hard. His heart gave out on him and their life together was cut short. That was over a year ago.

Linc wasn't sure, so he asked, "So, which one broke your heart?"

"Neither, I broke it, by settling. Don't misunderstand, Arlando was a good man, and I did love him, but I was looking for something in both of them that they didn't possess."

"Does that bring us back to the satisfying thing?"

Sonja laughed. "I think it goes a little deeper than that, but yes, that's part of it."

They sat munching on chips and dip just watching each other. It was the gun shots that broke their silence. They even heard a few fireworks going off. Linc and Sonja had just brought in the New Year together.

Linc got up from his seat, pulled Sonja from hers, and shifted her into his arms.

"Happy New Year to you, Sonja."

"Happy New Year to you, Linc."

Slowly, Linc kissed her, taking his time. He licked the salt from her lips before plunging inside her sweet mouth. As Sonja returned his kiss, something inside of Linc went haywire. Damn she felt so soft, and he delighted in the taste of her. Her lips were like a favorite dessert. Linc began an enticing slow grid, pushing against her softness. Linc felt Sonja moan his name inside his mouth, as she too pressed in closer.

"Oh baby." Linc heard his words as they floated from his mouth.

He picked Sonja up and carried her to the living room and situated them on the couch, positioning her on top of his body. He began to kiss her deeply, driving his tongue in and out of her mouth, tasting and teasing her. Sonja broke the kiss and began opening up his shirt. She ran her hands across his strong chest before she began her physical attack. Utilizing her hands and her tongue, she worked her way to his navel and back to his mouth once more.

Linc was just about to remove her top when another gunshot brought them both back to reality. Sonja jumped off of Linc's strong body and came to her feet.

"I'm…I'm sorry, Linc."

"Wait a minute, baby; we don't have to stop. I want you, girl, bad."

"I, I want you too, but let's be practical. You only want me for one night."

"Don't you want to know what it feels like to be pleased through and through? No one else needs to ever know. We can let it stay between the two of us. Satisfaction is a beautiful thing, baby. Let me please you, show you how it feels. Then once I've rocked you to sleep, I will leave. No strings, no regrets."

Linc studied Sonja's precious almond face for a moment. Then he realized what he was doing. He was practically begging her to be with him. Lincoln Stone had never begged any woman. Shit, they begged him. He started to re-button his shirt as he got up from the couch. Linc took Sonja by the hand.

"Thanks for the drink and for bring the New Year in with me. Funny, I've never spent New Year's with a woman before, never wanted to, but I enjoyed our time together."

Sonja walked him to the door. Before he slipped his shoes back on, he leaned in and gave her a kiss on the forehead. Sonja slowly closed her eyes and took in his scent. She let out a shallow breath as her body shook from need. She wasn't thinking straight. Maybe it was the liquor, but she wanted to know if he could satisfy her. For so many years her main focus had been her children. But tonight was going to be about her. As Linc turned, Sonja ran her hand down his arm and his body reacted to her touch. Quickly, he turned and seized her mouth as he ran a slow hand down her backside.

Softly Sonja spoke, "Satisfy me."

Linc went still as he looked deep into her big brown eyes. He took her in his arms.

"Baby, which way?"

Chapter 2

Sonja pointed Linc in the right direction, and soon they were standing beside her king size bed.

Linc stood still as Sonja undressed him. She took her time, Sonja was enjoying the sights. There wasn't one body part in particular that impressed her more than another, everything about him was exquisite. Linc may have been forty, but his body would make any young man head back to the gym to work a little harder on his frame. His ginger skin was very soft, his muscles were very well defined, and his stomach was firm. His legs! All Sonja could think was "powerful". Panic ran through her. What was he going to think when he got a look at her body? She was a thirty-eight year old, mother of three, and all three were cesarean births. All she could think of was her scar. Linc sensed her tension.

Linc placed a tender finger under her chin. "What's wrong, baby? Have you changed your mind?"

"I'm afraid that once you've seen my scar, you will change your mind. Linc, the women you are used to being with are much younger than me. And it's been told, that you don't deal with women who have children. Maybe I should stop this before I embarrass myself."

He kissed her gently and began to remove her clothing. "I want you, baby, all of you."

After helping Sonja step out of her pants, Linc began kissing her. He started with her forehead then went south. When he reached her scar, he paused. First, he ran his strong hand across her stomach, down to her scar, where he stopped and used one finger to trace it from left to right. Sonja shivered from his skillful touch. Sweetly, Linc kissed her there before placing his face against her stomach. He held his head there for a few moments, loving the feel of her skin, and the way her hands felt as she ran them through his hair. Linc looked up at Sonja.

"I love your scar, baby. It's a part of who you are."

Sonja felt a single tear fall, and it landed on Linc's shoulder.

"Get in the bed, honey."

Sonja did as he asked. He climbed in beside her and pulled her under his strong body. He knew she was ready, he could smell her pleasing aroma. It was hypnotic. Linc reached for his pants and retrieved his wallet. Inside he found three condoms. He sat two on the nightstand and covered his hard steel with the other.

"I hope you are ready for this."

He didn't give her a chance to respond. Swiftly, Linc kissed her as he took his position between her legs. Taking Sonja's hand, Linc helped her guide him in.

As Linc slid inside her heat, Sonja felt a jolt of pleasure rush through her insides. Linc heard Sonja softly whimper.

"Am I hurting you, Sonja?"

"No, it's just been a long time, and, you just feel so good."

Linc kissed her. "Good, because I'm going deeper, baby; this ride is just starting."

As Linc plunged in deeper, he felt her close around him. He trembled with pleasure. In his journey toward satisfying Sonja, deep within her essence, Linc had stumble upon something he'd never felt before, and he was enjoying it!

"Oh Lord, baby!"

Linc began his mission as he drove in deep and forceful. Much to his surprise, Sonja kept up with his rhythm. He was supplying her with a dominant driving energy, and she responded by requesting more. Sonja's body was tingling with need, and she couldn't stand it any longer. Just as she called out his name, Linc felt her begin to unravel, and he thought he was losing his mind. Linc couldn't hold out any longer, so he seized her hips and raised them up higher so he could take them home.

She wrapped her arms tightly around Linc's neck and drew her body up as she tightened her legs around his waist. Linc brought her up with him, and they both found closure. Sonja called out his name once more just before she shattered into a million pieces. Linc arched his back as he let out a roar that was music to Sonja's ears.

It took him a few minutes to regain control as he lay on top of Sonja's very satisfied body. Linc had developed his skills as a playa at a very young age. Pleasing a beautiful woman came natural for him. Looking down at her as he moved his large frame from her, he could tell he had pleased her. But, she had done something no other woman had. She had pleased him, too.

"Damn, baby, where you been all my life?"

Just before Sonja drifted off to sleep, she replied, "Searching for you."

Linc pulled Sonja in close, cradled her in his arms and watched her sleep. Linc knew it was time for him to leave, but he just couldn't bring himself to do it. Not yet, not until he got another taste of paradise. He kissed her close to her ear and closed his eyes.

A few hours later, Sonja awoke when she felt a strong arm pulling her closer. Turning, she looked directly into Linc's light brown eyes.

"Hey, love, did I wake you?"

Sonja enjoyed the feel of Linc's strong arms around her.

"That's okay, it's nice waking up in your arms."

Linc began pulling her in closer. "Come here, love, I have something that belongs to you."

Sonja looked on as Linc moved the covers back to reveal his strong member calling out to her. She turned and grabbed a condom from the table and swiftly shielded him before she climbed his shaft and started round two.

His loving was so slow, tender and caring. Sonja had to keep reminding herself that they were only playing make believe. Gently, Sonja kissed him as she found completion once again. They were still for a while, but then Sonja decided playtime was over. Sonja began to move away from Linc, but Linc had other plans.

"Linc, we should stop."

"Wait, I just want to hold you a little while longer."

Sonja thought perhaps Linc was extra passionate towards her because he felt sorry for her. She questioned his spoken desire to be with her longer, but then Sonja decided that she was going to enjoy every moment they shared.

"Okay, give me a minute. I will be right back."

"Hurry back. And Sonja?"

"Yes, Linc?"

"No regrets, right?"

"Not a one!" Sonja blew Linc a kiss as she grabbed his shirt and put it on before she walked out of the bedroom.

Linc rested his arm behind his head and smiled as he remembered the fabulous sensation he felt, buried so deep inside of Sonja. He was turned on by the way she responded to his touch the first time and each time after. Suddenly, as if he were being watched, Linc turned and observed his reflection in the mirror. What the hell was he doing? He was a playa, not some love sick punk. No, he would never go down that road again. Connie had taught him a very valuable lesson. All he promised Sonja was a night of passion, and he had delivered. It was time for him to get back to his life, and let her get back to her kids. Linc looked at the clock. It was almost noon. Then he looked at the table by the bed; there was one more condom.

Linc spoke to his reflection in the mirror as if he needed to explain. "Why should we waste it? One more taste, and then I'm gone."

Sonja stood in front of the mirror in her bathroom looking closely at the woman staring back at her. For some reason, she thought she would feel uncomfortable. At first she couldn't believe what she had done. Sleeping with a stranger! With a wide smile spread across her face, Sonja gave her reflection a nod of approval. What Linc Stone had done to her body will forever be etched in her mind. What a man, what a man! Knowing that she would never see him again saddened her, but Sonja knew she would never regret the time shared with him.

When Sonja returned to the room, Linc was anxiously waiting for her. As she approached the bed, Linc pulled the blankets back to reveal his manhood already sheathed and in full bloom.

Linc rocked Sonja back to sleep, and then eased out of bed. He went into the bathroom and took a quick shower. He needed to leave before she woke back up. He was wrestling with his emotions as he carefully washed away what they had shared. He didn't want to leave her, ever. But he was a playa, not a staya. He wasn't meant to be one woman's man. And he sure as hell wasn't meant to be anyone's daddy.

Linc made his way through Sonja's house, collecting his things. Goodness, one would think he lived there. It seemed he had left something in every room! Linc had broken so many rules with this woman. In his handbook, a playa never cuddles, and he never spends the night. Allowing a woman to wake up in your arms gave them too much to hope for.

Slowly closing the front door behind him, he stood there for a moment, wishing he had gone back and said goodbye. Standing there facing the door, Linc didn't see or hear the car pull into the driveway.

Out of the car jumped fourteen-year-old Matthew, and Jeffrey, he was eleven. And right behind them was Terrell and Tiffany. Tiffany noticed the SUV in her mother's driveway first, then the man standing in front of the door. She had just finished talking to her mother on the phone, informing her they were right outside. Tiffany knew she had roused her mother out of her sleep, so she was sure her mom wasn't aware that she had a guest.

Linc was so deep in thought at first he didn't hear Tiffany talking to him.

"Excuse me, sir, but can I help you with something?"

Linc turned to find a light-skinned, pretty young woman, who looked like a younger version of Sonja standing before him. Next to her was a dark-skinned young man. Hanging onto each of her arms was two little fellows.

"Hi, I'm Lincoln Stone. I'm a new friend of Sonja's. I was on my way out of town, and I just wanted to say goodbye to her."

Tiffany held out her hand to Linc. "Hi, I'm Sonja's daughter, Tiffany. This is my husband, Terrell. And these two are my brothers, Matthew and Jeffrey."

Linc spoke to everyone. He wasn't surprised to find Sonja's children were very well behaved.

Tiffany used her key to let them inside. Once inside, she called out to her mother. Linc wasn't sure why he was still there. He should have been on the road hours ago. But he couldn't get his feet to move, not until he looked at her again.

Sonja came around the corner, calling out to her boys. There was so much love in her voice and in her eyes when she looked at her children. And then she noticed Linc. He was still standing by the door.

Tiffany caught the surprised look on her mother's face. "Mom, this poor man was standing outside knocking when we pulled up. You must have been passed out in here!"

"Yes, I was. Sorry, Linc, I didn't know you were outside."

Linc cleared his throat. "That's okay. I just wanted to say goodbye. Well, I have, so now I guess I will be going."

Tiffany knew something was going on between this fine man and her mother, so she spoke up. "Don't go just yet, we ordered pizza! Please stay and have some with us."

Tiffany turned to her husband. "Terrell, help the boys get the games hooked back up, please."

Terrell followed Matthew and Jeffrey to their room. Tiffany stood there looking at her mom for a moment.

"Mom, I'm going to go back and help Terrell and the boys."

"Okay, honey."

When Tiffany was out of sight, Linc spoke first. "I'm sorry. I thought I would be gone before your family made it back home."

"That's okay, I'm glad you stayed to say goodbye."

"Yes, me too." Linc looked back in the direction Sonja's children headed. "You have a fine family, how old?"

"Matthew is fourteen and Jeffrey is eleven-years-old. My daughter Tiffany is nineteen, and her husband Terrell is twenty-one. They just got married a few months ago."

Linc looked surprised. "Really, and you are okay with it?"

"If I want to be a part of my daughter's life, I have to be. Terrell is a good person. He will take good care of my baby."

Linc reached inside his wallet and pulled out one of his business cards and handed it to Sonja.

"Here, take my card. Give me a call, if you ever want to talk."

Sonja took the card and studied it for a moment before putting it in the pocket of the green terry cloth robe she was wearing. She then excused herself. She needed to take a quick shower.

Linc stayed for another hour or so playing on the X-box with Terrell and the boys while eating pizza. He was very sad when he had to leave, but it was time to get back to his life; the fast life.

Sonja walked Linc to the door while Tiffany and Terrell took the boys in the kitchen to help clean up.

Linc wrapped his arms around Sonja and hugged her tight. "No regrets, remember?"

"Never, I'm sure we will never meet up again, but I will remember our time together for the rest of my life. Thank you, Linc Stone, for showing me how it feels to be satisfied."

Linc kissed her hard and long before he made himself let her go. He walked out the door and begged his body not to betray him. All he wanted to do was go back inside, sweep her off her feet, carry her back to the bedroom and go as deep as her body could stand. And stay there forever.

Linc programmed his system in his truck for home. He had a long ride back to Indianapolis ahead of him. Linc had told Sonja he was headed for Kalamazoo, but that wasn't the truth. He just didn't want Chad to get his paws on Sonja. Believe it or not, Linc didn't plan on sleeping with Sonja. For the life of him, he could seem to control his emotions when it came to her.

At a young age, he found that it was easier to not get involved with women who had children. Linc knew that he didn't want to have children of his own. But, there was something about this woman that caused him to do things…things he'd didn't plan on doing.

Chapter 3

As Linc traveled down the busy highway, his mind lingered on Sonja and her family. She had a great family; he felt she was blessed. For just a moment, Linc pondered on what a relationship with Sonja would be like. He quickly tossed the thought out of his mind. Although he would never say it aloud, Linc felt he was more like his mother than he cared to admit. Carrying around that bit of knowledge, Linc knew he never wanted a significant other or kids. He never wanted to be a disappointment to either of them.

When Linc was around twenty-four years old, he convinced himself that having a vasectomy would be the answer to all of his fears. Only then did he feel safe. But before he had the procedure, there had been two women that Linc had unprotected sex with. Linc had just begun to build his financial portfolio and was worth a little paper. This gold digger had sniffed him out, claiming she was carrying Linc's child. With the aid of his good friend and lawyer, Hunter Merrill, the truth was revealed. The young woman wasn't carrying Linc's baby, in fact, she wasn't pregnant.

The second encounter was with his ex-girlfriend, Connie. He wasn't worried about Connie getting pregnant; she had always been on the pill. Linc had run into Connie a few years after their relationship ended. He was in his hometown, Gary, Indiana, looking at a building. He was thinking about buying it. As he was exiting the building, he came face-to-face with Connie. It was clear that Connie and her man had experienced a falling out, and she needed someone to hold her.

Connie had always thought she could control Linc with sex. But Linc had since joined the players club and had become a different person. Linc bedded her that night, and like all the rest of the women he had encountered, he had her begging him for more. Instead of giving into her needs, he left her lying in bed, pleading with him to give her another chance. He had long gotten over Connie; he just needed to see for himself that her stuff was just like any other woman's. He could take it or leave it.

Linc shook off those bad memories. He placed his ear piece in and began listening to his messages on his cell phone. Most of the calls were from women. There was one from Hunter. He asked Linc to contact him as soon as possible. He needed to talk to Linc about his property in Chicago. And then, there was the call from his younger brother. That was the one that got Linc's attention. Linc's little brother, Kamrin Stone, hadn't spoken to him in months. Linc had pissed Kamrin off when he told Kamrin his wife was a whore.

Since they were young, Linc had always lovingly referred to Kamrin as LB, short for little brother. Linc never trusted Kamrin's wife, Adriane, and decided to check on things while LB was out of town. It was just last year when Linc caught Adriane with another man. Adriane was entertaining her gentlemen friends in their home.

Much to Adriane's surprise, Linc had a key to the house. So when he used that key to enter his brother's home, he found Adriane and one of her male friends getting it on, on Kamrin's newly carpeted living room floor.

Linc knew that he wouldn't have to tell his brother about Adriane, she was going to tell on herself, every reckless cheat did. And sure enough, before Linc laid his eyes on Kamrin, she had spilled the beans. But she was a clever little witch. Adriane made up some ridiculous story, and Kamrin bought right into it.

Kamrin didn't approve of Linc's lifestyle. Kamrin was like their father. He wanted to find one woman to be with and spend the rest of his life making her happy. Unlike Kamrin, Linc chose to spend the rest of his life pleasing himself. When Linc tried to school his brother about Adriane, Kamrin became furious. He told Linc he didn't believe him. Kamrin told his brother that he trusted his wife, and if Linc had a problem with that, then he shouldn't come around anymore.

Linc loved his little brother, but Kamrin was too much like their father. So, Linc decided to bide his time. Linc hired a detective to capture Adriane in a few of her special moments. So when Kamrin finally came back to his senses, Linc would have what he needed to make sure the witch didn't take his brother to the cleaners.

Linc spoke to his on-star system. "Call LB."

It responded, "Calling Kamrin Stone."

The phone rang a few times, but there was no answer. Linc told himself not to get too worked up; Kamrin was fine. He would just try later.

Linc decided to call Hunter. He wanted to find out what was going on with his building in Chicago. Linc and Hunter met at a party many years ago, right after Hunter finished law school. Back then, Hunter was the ripe age of twenty-five, and a new member of the playas club. Linc had taken him under his wing. Women called Hunter "The Black Zorro." If a woman was lucky enough to be chosen by Hunter, he most defiantly left his mark.

Hunter practiced law because he enjoyed the challenge, the thrill he always got after winning his case. He knew from the start that it was going to take long hours and sleepless nights, and he enjoyed to challenge. Hunter didn't have to be concerned about money, he came from money. Hunter Merrill was born with a silver spoon in his mouth. He was a sophisticated, wealthy, remarkably handsome young black man, with a passion for law, every aspect of it. He was knowledgeable in numerous areas of the law and able to practice in five states. The man knew what he was doing.

Hunter and Linc have been hanging tight for well over ten years. They were like brothers. Linc and Kamrin were the only clients Hunter dealt directly with.

Hunter picked up on the second ring.

"What's up, Hunter?"

"Hey, Linc, man, I thought I would catch you at home this morning. Where you been?"

Linc and Hunter laughed. Hunter knew Linc had rules, and there were two he swore to never break. The first was he never let women stay at his house. The second was Linc never brought the New Year in with a woman. Linc felt that doing so made the women think there would be more between them.

"Shut up, man! Talk to me about Chicago!"

"Damn, man, she must have been good!"

"Yeah, it was your sister! Now can we talk about business?"

"You lucky I don't have a sister."

Linc and Hunter laughed.

"Right, I guess that means it's none of your business! But if you must know, DAMN! Now tell me about Chicago."

Linc's body shuddered from just the thought of his love making with Sonja.

"Ha! That's what I'm talking about, my dawg! But for real man, I got a call from some woman on a crusade to help the inner city children. She wants to talk to you about the possibility of letting them use some of the space in your Chicago building for the kids. The woman that's representing the group, her name is...Tuesdae Parker. I told her I would talk to you, and if you were interested, we would set up a meeting."

"That's cool. Call her back and see when she wants to meet."

"Good, I will talk to you in a few days."

Linc finished his call. He only stopped to gas up once and then he took it on in. When he finally made it home, it was close to 9 p.m. As Linc pulled into his yard, he noticed a truck parked by his garage. As he made his way closer, Linc realized his guest was Kamrin.

Kamrin stepped out of his SUV and grabbed his bag. He waited for Linc to put his truck in the garage. Linc knew something was wrong by the look on his brother's face.

"Hey, LB, what's going on? What brings you out my way?"

Linc took a good look at his brother. Kamrin's eyes were red; he had been crying.

"What's wrong, man? Talk to me."

"You were right, and I was wrong."

"Come on; let's go inside so we can talk." Linc placed his arm around his brother's shoulder and guided him inside the house.

"Why didn't you let yourself in? You still have your key, right?"

"After the way I talk to you the last time, I wasn't sure if you would want me here."

"You and I are family. I will never let anything or anyone come between you and me. I know you didn't mean those things you said to me. I was just giving you time to cool off. Now tell me what happened."

"I caught her. She had some guy waiting, watching for me to leave the house. When she thought I was gone, she rushed him inside. I parked around the block and entered the house through the basement window."

"Well, what brought on all this detective work?"

"A lot of things I've been trying to ignore for the past few years. Like the phone calls, the shopping trips, her not wanting to sleep with me. You know that kind of stuff. The stuff you warned me about."

"Where is she now? Not in your house I hope!"

"Hell no! I tossed her ass out last week. She's hired some fancy lawyer, and she thinks she is going to take half of everything I own."

After their parents died, Linc sold the family house and put some of the money into certificates and stocks and bonds. Linc had been securing a future for him and his brother. They also had their father's insurance policy from his work place. Linc used their parents' life insurance policies to put him and his brother through college. So, the Stone brothers were well off.

"Like hell! Your big brother has got something for her ass!"

Linc walked over to where his brother was standing and gave him a brotherly hug.

"Don't worry, LB; everything is going to be fine."

Linc's heart hurt for his brother. This thing with Adriane brought back too many bad memories, memories of that crazy morning. It was the morning everything went wrong for the Stone family.

Linc was twenty and Kamrin was eighteen. Linc's father had worked overnight, and his mother was out doing Lord knows what. Linc had stayed out all night with his girlfriend, Connie, and was trying to beat his father home. He had made it in the yard just before his father pulled in the driveway. His plan was to let his father get inside and begin his routine, and then he would have his brother let him in.

That's not how it went down. Just as Leroy Stone got out of his car, he heard the neighbor lady scream. Linc's dad thought someone had broken in and was trying to hurt her. So being the kind-hearted man he was he went to aid her. But when Leroy entered the house, he found his neighbor holding a gun on her husband and Leroy's half-naked wife.

Linc could still hear the woman screaming. *"I told you, Herb, if I caught you with that bitch again, I would kill the both of you."*

Apparently the woman had caught Deborah Stone and her husband together before, and he must have promised to leave her alone.

Linc had made his way to the neighbor's window to get a better look. There she was standing with that smirk on her face. Deborah cared for no one but herself. Linc's father was trying to talk to his neighbor. He was begging her to put the gun down.

The woman told Deborah if she didn't wipe that smile off her face, it was going to be her last. The woman's husband tried to say something to her, but the sound of his voice caused her to snap.

The woman pointed the gun at her husband and shot. Then she turned it on Linc's mother. Just as she was about to pull the trigger, Linc's father jumped in front of his wife. But it didn't matter. The bullet went right through the both of them. After the woman realized what she had done, she turned the gun on herself.

Linc ran in the house; he needed to help his father. He dropped down on the floor and pulled his father into his arms.

"Son, cover your mother up; don't let people see her like that."

Linc looked at his father with disbelief. What did he care how she looked? If it wasn't for her, none of this would have happened. But out of respect for his father,

Linc found a blanket and covered his mother's body.

"Son, I love you and your brother. Please promise me you will take care of your brother."

Tears streamed down Linc's face. "I love you, too, Daddy. I promise."

Linc knew his dad wasn't going to make it. He buried his head in his father's chest and just cried. The next thing he remembered was the police officer trying to pry Linc's father from his grip. They guided the severely traumatized Linc to the back of the squad car, where he found his brother sitting, crying. Linc's face and his shirt were covered in his father's blood.

The woman's husband died. Linc and Kamrin lost their mother and father. But somehow, the woman survived. She's spending the rest of her life in jail, because Deborah Stone didn't know how to appreciate what she had in her husband and her two sons.

No, Linc wasn't going to let Adriane win. Hell no. Only this time no one was going to die.

♥

It took weeks for Hunter and Adriane's lawyer to finally meet. Once they met, Hunter knew the case was going to be a breeze. With Hunter on the case, it didn't take long and Kamrin's divorce papers were filed. Linc had provided enough damaging evidence of her extramarital affairs that the judge wouldn't need much time to make his ruling. Adriane and her lawyer knew she didn't have a leg to stand on once they were presented with the evidence Linc had provided.

After discovering that she would have to fight Kamrin for the house, she decided against it. Kamrin and his lawyer offered her a onetime alimony payment. Adriane took it, but after it was all said and done she thought she would take one more shot at Kamrin. So, after leaving the courthouse, Adriane followed Kamrin out of the building, pleading with him to give her another chance; she even promised Kamrin they could have a child, if he took her back. The way she performed, it was sad. Kamrin and Adriane had been married for five years, but whenever the subject of children came up in the past, she was never ready. But now that she was being thrown out on the streets, Adriane was ready to give Kamrin the child he had been wanting for so many years. Kamrin didn't miss a beat when he told her she couldn't pay him to touch her again.

Kamrin put the house up for sale; he didn't want to sleep in that house ever again. Thanks to Hunter and Linc, Adriane never would. He took a leave of absence from his job as a human resources manager at one of the major car companies. He wanted to hang out with his big brother for a while. After making sure the sale of Kamrin's house was in good hands, Linc, Kamrin and Hunter drove to Chicago for their meeting with Ms. Tuesdae Parker.

♥

They had arrived in Chicago two days early. It was the first week in February, and there was a slight chill in the air. The three men checked into a five star hotel and prepared to party. Linc and Hunter were going to make sure Kamrin had a good time. Armed with a good supply of protection, it was party time. None of the men had any problems picking up women; the three were like magnets when it came to women. Linc was sophisticated, Kamrin possessed a boyish charm, and Hunter was dark and mysterious.

Linc had been so busy for the last few weeks helping his brother that he hadn't found the time to think about just how much he missed Sonja. That is, until he got in his hotel room and found a few moments of quiet time. Linc stepped out of the shower and put on his robe. He picked up his cell phone to make sure he hadn't missed any calls. No, Sonja hadn't called. Linc was shocked. Normally, by now, any other woman would have blown his phone up! Especially if he put it on them like he had put it on Sonja.

Man, his feelings were hurt. Linc wasn't going to stand for this. She was just one woman. He was going to go out with Kamrin and Hunter, and when he came back to his room, he was going to have a young, fine honey that would be ready and willing to wrap her fine young legs around him. That's all he needed to get back in the swing of things.

Hunter suggested that they eat first then hit a few clubs. The first club they stopped in, they found seats at the bar. Hunter told the bartender to keep the cognac coming. Every time Linc thought about Sonja, he would find another woman to toy with. Linc and Hunter were dancing with two little honeys, and Kamrin was collecting phone numbers left and right. Kamrin was having a good time.

Kamrin wasn't used to all of this, but he did enjoy hanging out with his brother. He always wondered how Linc did it. Why didn't Linc want to have one special woman in his life? Even though Kamrin was going to enjoy being with one of these women tonight, his heart was still set on finding Miss Right!

Two hours later, the men were on their way back to the hotel with cuties on hand. By the time Linc made it back to his room, the liquor was in control, and he was lit. The young woman with him couldn't wait to get him in the bed. Linc had never in his life had a problem pleasing a desirable woman, but every time he got ready to kiss her, he thought of Sonja.

Linc was trying hard to focus on the young beauty in front of him, but it wasn't working. He was starting to get pissed off. The young woman began kissing Linc, but he felt like pushing her away. What was wrong with him, maybe he just needed to throw some water on his face.

Linc took the woman by the hands and gently pushed her back. "Wow, sorry. I think maybe the cognac is taking over. Just let me go run some water over my face."

"Sure, honey; I'll be waiting for you in the bed."

Linc headed for the bathroom. On the way, he felt his phone vibrating. His pulse began to race. Linc just knew it was Sonja. Quickly, he entered the bathroom and closed the door tight.

"Hello?"

The woman's voice was unfamiliar to him. He didn't care who she was, she wasn't Sonja.

"Linc, hey, I was wondering what you were doing tonight."

Instead of answering, he just hung up. Linc pressed his back against the bathroom door. He was mad. Who did Sonja Davis think she was? He was Linc Stone! Linc pounded Sonja's phone number in and waited for her to answer. The phone rang three times.

A sleepy voice answered. "Hello?"

His voice was sharp and crisp. "Yeah, were you busy?"

"Linc, where are you?"

Her voice was groggy, and it causing things on his body to move. Linc was getting very upset. He didn't like the way she could make his body heat up with just her voice.

"Oh, so now you want to act like you care. I've been gone for well over a month, and you haven't called me once."

The young lady in the other room was starting to get a little concerned, so she went to the bathroom door and knocked.

"Linc, are you all right in there. I'm still waiting for you to come to bed."

Linc tried to put his hand over the phone, but he was too late.

"I will be right out. I'm talking to my baby. Get away from the damn door."

Sonja heard the woman's voice and began to feel sick inside. But she knew she had no right to, he wasn't her man. Her words came out crisp.

"Linc, hang up. Your date is in bed waiting for you."

"You know what, Sonja? You're right. I'm a playa for life, baby. Bye."

Linc stepped out of the bathroom and took one look at the sweet young thang stretched across his bed. He knew it wasn't going to work. He told himself it was because he had a little too much to drink. But he knew the truth.

"Look, this just ain't gonna happen tonight. Let me call you a cab."

"Are you sure? I can do something to help you get ready."

"No, baby girl. If he ain't willing, it ain't gonna happen."

"Did I do something wrong?"

"No, I think it's the liquor. Some other time, okay?"

Linc called down and had the doorman get a cab for the young lady. Then he took a nice, long, hot shower, climbed into bed, and dreamed about Sonja.

After that incident, Linc spent the next night in his hotel room, alone. He told Hunter and Kamrin he had some things he needed to take care of. Linc didn't want to go through another night like his last one.

The next day, the three men were sitting in the restaurant waiting on Ms. Tuesdae Parker to arrive. Linc and Hunter were going over some papers while Kamrin was being propositioned by the waitress. All three men were handsome, but Kamrin's boyish charm sometimes just took over.

Kamrin noticed her first; she was dazzling. The maître d' pointed Tuesdae in the right direction. When she arrived at the table, Kamrin was the first one to jump up and pull out a seat for her. Ms Tuesdae Parker was five foot five, and she was a brick house! Her short curly strawberry blonde hairstyle fit her perfect round face. And in her tiny nose there was a wee diamond stud nose ring.

Linc and Hunter looked at one another as Kamrin gave them the "girl is mine" look! Tuesdae stopped at the table and introduced herself to the men.

"Good afternoon, gentlemen. I'm Tuesdae Parker."

She then took the seat Kamrin offered.

Hunter spoke. "Ms. Parker, I'm Hunter Merrill, and this is my client, Lincoln Stone. And the gentleman seated next to you is Mr. Stone's brother, Kamrin Stone. It's nice to finally meet you."

"Thank you. Mr. Stone, Mr. Stone, Mr. Merrill, it's nice to meet all of you."

Tuesdae didn't waste any time, she got straight to the point. "Mr. Stone, I have written up a proposal for you. Along with the proposal, I have letters from around five different businesses who would be willing to rent spaces from you. But before you look at any of this, I would like a chance to pitch my organization's proposal."

Before Tuesdae could begin, the waitress stopped at the table to take everyone's orders. Once the orders were taken, Tuesdae began.

"Our organization is called Save our Sons and Daughters, or S.S.D. I was hoping we could occupy the bottom half of the building, use some of the space for computer labs. Fix up an area and use it as a gym. You know, give the kids something to do after school, even in the summertime. Help keep them off the streets."

Tuesdae went on for a few more moments explaining her program and what they plan to achieve.

Kamrin was the first to speak up. "Linc, she has some good ideas, what do you say?"

"I say, draft up the layout of what you're talking about. Give Hunter some time to check out some of these businesses that have expressed an interest in occupying building space. And then we can talk."

After lunch, Kamrin offered to escort Tuesdae to her car. She accepted. Hunter told Linc he was going to hang out in the Windy City and get started. Linc waited for Kamrin to come back inside the restaurant. As Kamrin entered, he sported a huge grin. Tuesdae had accepted Kamrin's invitation to dinner. Hunter told Linc not to worry about Kamrin, he would keep an eye on him.

A few hours later, Linc was on a plane headed for South Bend. When Linc got off the plane, he rented a car. He couldn't take it any longer, he was going to Dowagiac.

Chapter 4

As Linc rolled into town, he noticed a young man with a cart full of flowers and plants. Linc pulled up next to him. The guy looked a little chilly as he sipped on something hot. Linc was surprised to see him sitting out there; it was still February, too cold to be selling flowers from a cart.

"Good morning, sir, can I interest you in some flowers for your valentine?"

Linc automatically thought about Sonja. Sonja wasn't his, but he wanted to buy her a rose anyway.

Linc handed the guy two large bills and suggested that maybe he should take the rest of the day off. Go someplace warm!

♥

Sonja had just returned home after transporting her boys to school. She stepped out of her sweats and put on her robe. She was in her bedroom getting ready to apply her make-up when she heard the front doorbell. As Sonja reached the door, she looked through the peephole. Sonja couldn't believe her eyes. It was Linc! Slowly she opened the door.

"Linc, what are you doing here?"

"Hey, love, aren't you going to invite me inside? It's cold out here!"

Sonja looked him up and down. She noticed how tired he looked, but the man still looked good enough to eat. Under his coat, Linc was wearing a tan wool jacket with a button down shirt and a pair of blue jeans. Sonja could smell his persuasive cologne.

"Come on in."

"Thanks. So you got the boys off to school, huh?"

"Are you spying on me?" Sonja didn't budge. The hallway was as far as this man was going. "I'm right in the middle of getting ready for work. Why are you here?"

Linc could tell she was trying hard to remain upset with him. "Look, I'm sorry about the phone call. I'd been drinking. It's your fault though."

"Excuse me?"

"I've been hurting ever since I left you well over a month ago."

Linc moved closer to Sonja and pulled her into his arms. He kissed her sweetly. Then Linc gently took Sonja's small hand and ran it over his bulge.

"Love, I'm hurting, and you are the only one who can make it better."

Linc moved his mouth to cover Sonja's once again, as she took over caressing him, trying to ease his pain. Linc stepped out of his shoes and dropped his coat on the floor. He picked Sonja up and carried her to the bedroom.

Linc made quick work of getting out of his things, and then removing Sonja's robe, making love to her was a must. Protecting them , he wasted no time covering her body with his own, Linc kissed her as he drove inside her body. As he found the right tempo that would bring satisfaction to both he kissed her again, moaning a sigh of relief in Sonja's starving mouth.

As Linc made his way deep into her center, he began to increase the tempo of his movements. Only then could he feel his whole body start to calm down.

"Mmm love, you are so good. You don't know how many times I've thought about us doing this."

Sonja knew she was playing a dangerous game. Linc was not a man she could have, and she didn't want to share him. But he felt so good inside her. This was going to be the last time.

Sonja placed her hands on Linc's butt, and urged him to increase his movement as she kissed him. The kiss was so intense Sonja wondered if Linc felt how it had come straight from her heart . After an intense workout of lovemaking, they found release multiple times before Linc was content.

She looked at the clock, and it was well after eight. She should already be at work. Sonja jumped out of bed and made her way around the room gathering up her clothes and heading for the bathroom to take a quick shower. It was forty-five minutes later when she re-entered the bedroom to check on Linc.

"Linc, I'm leaving. I have to get to work."

"Come give me my kiss."

Sonja stopped in front of her bed, and Linc reached his arms out for her.

With mischief sparkling in his light brown eyes, he spoke to her. "Come here, baby."

Sonja didn't miss it. "No, Linc; I'm already late!"

"Okay." Linc sat up and gave her a long hot kiss. Then he ran a gentle finger down her chin. "Thank you. I needed you really bad."

Sonja tilted her head to the side, trying to figure this man out. "Linc, I thought we were only going to have one night."

"We were, but I had a craving. No other woman was going to satisfy it. Don't worry, I think I'm full."

Sonja looked hurt as she playfully swatted at Linc's strong arm. "Thanks a lot."

"No, baby, I didn't mean it that way. Stop playing , you know what I meant. If it's all good, I think I will take a quick nap before I get back on the road. I promise to be gone before you get home."

She wanted him to stay, but she knew better than to ask. Instead, she nodded. She watched as he made himself comfortable in her bed. She stood and headed for the door. Then she stopped and turned to face Linc once more.

"Linc, I know it's really none of my business. But, the other night when you called...did you sleep with that woman?"

"No." Linc rolled over and closed his eyes. He had to bite his tongue to keep from giving her a full explanation. Sonja was just another woman that he slept with, and when he leaves her today, they won't see each other again.

Linc could feel Sonja looking at him, but he wouldn't turn around. Finally she turned and walked out.

♥

When Sonja made it to work, she had a message from Nancy. Nancy was looking for a particular file, and she was sure it was in the Dowagiac office. She needed Sonja to find it and fax it over. Then she wanted her to make copies and send the copies by FedEx®. It sounded like a simple task, but Sonja's mind was on a big bad wolf back at her house, sleeping in her bed, so she was having trouble finding the file. Once she found it, everything else fell right into place.

Sonja worked straight through lunch. She wanted to get as much done as she could. She always left work by three p.m. Sonja had to make sure she was off in time to pick Matthew and Jeffrey up from school. Matthew always walked to Jeffrey's school to get his brother, and Sonja would pick them up and head home with her boys.

As Sonja approached her house, she noticed Linc's car was gone. She felt sadness come over her. But Sonja knew Linc's leaving was for the best. Once she and her boys were inside, she prepared them a snack and went to the freezer and removed something to prepare for dinner. As the boys ate their snacks and began their home-work, Sonja went in her bedroom to change her clothes.

Entering the room, Sonja noticed Linc had changed her sheets and placed a single rose on her pillow! Sonja picked up the rose and delighted in its aroma. A few seconds later, she observed Linc's sports jacket draped on the back of her vanity chair. She sat the rose back on the bed and picked up his jacket. Sonja put it around her shoulders and hugged it close to her body before hanging it in her closet.

♥

Linc made his way inside his house. First he checked his phone for messages. One message was from a young lady that had been trying to get "Stoned" for months. His initial reaction was to delete the message. Linc started questioning his reasons for wanting to do so. If he hadn't known any better, Linc would think he was in love… hell no. Linc picked up the phone as he shook off those crazy thoughts.

Punching in the number, Linc returned the young lady's call. They spoke casually before making plans to meet for dinner that evening. Linc didn't want to go out, but he knew if he didn't get back into the swing of things, this thing he had, or didn't have with Sonja was going to drive him mad. Deciding that he was doing the right thing, Linc went into his bathroom and prepared his bath water.

♥

Sonja and her boys had a nice semi-quiet evening. After dinner, the boys helped her wash the dishes, then she allowed them to bring their Xbox game out and hook it up to the big screen television. As the boys played, Sonja read a book. The doorbell began to ring, and Sonja looked over at the clock. It was almost seven o'clock in the evening. When Sonja got to the door, she looked through the peep hole and found her neighbor, Dexter. Dexter was a fine, thirty-five-year old brotha. He had been out of town for a few days, but he wanted to let Sonja and the boys know he was back.

Dexter and her last husband, Arlando, had been close friends. Now Dexter mowed the lawn and kept her driveway plowed in the winter for his friend's family. After Arlando died, Dexter made it a point to always be available to Sonja and her children.

"Hey, Dex, when did you get back in town?"

The boys ran to the door when they heard Dexter's voice. "Dexter, come inside and play a game with us!"

"Long as it's alright with your mom."

"Sure, come on in. Have you eaten already? I made beef stew."

"Is that what's smelling so good? Give me a big bowl!"

Sonja smiled at her friend as she headed for the kitchen to fix him up. Dexter visited with them until well after nine in the evening, and then went to his home next door.

At the end of the evening, Sonja kissed her boys goodnight and headed for her bedroom to read for a while longer. Sonja read for a few hours, but she kept thinking about Linc. What had he meant when he said he had a craving that only she could fill? Sonja would venture to believe, Linc could have found a number of women to satisfy his craving. But Sonja was glad that this time he had picked her. She looked at the clock and noticed it was after eleven p.m. She pulled the card from the drawer in the nightstand and dialed the first number she found. She got a recording.

"This is Lincoln Stone; leave a message."

"Hi, Linc, just wanted to say goodnight."

Sonja quickly hung up the phone and turned out the light. As she waited for sleep to come, Sonja promised herself that she would not let this lead to a broken heart.

♥

Inside the elegant restaurant, Linc sat across from a very stunning young woman named Vera. He didn't know her last name, he didn't want to. Her green eyes sparkled when she smiled, and her shiny auburn hair looked smooth as it brushed her shoulders. She was around thirty-years old and an extremely hot little number. Linc told himself that he was going to have a memorable time peeling that little dress off her tasty petite body.

They finished dinner, and Vera offered to supply Linc with dessert at her apartment. Linc was getting a little worried; his partner down there wasn't responding like he should. What was the deal? This woman was fine, and she was ready to knock some boots!

Inside Vera's apartment, she offered Linc a drink as she hung up their coats. Vera got Linc a shot of whiskey straight up, and she poured herself a glass of white wine. Linc sat down on the couch and knocked back the shot of whiskey, then sat the glass on the coffee table.

Vera went to the couch and placed her dainty body on Linc's lap and began to cover his mouth with hers. She worked her tongue in an out of his mouth a few times before she pushed up her dress so she could straddled him better. Enjoying the way he tasted, Vera decided she needed more, so she began to work her jewel over him, hoping to get him prepared.

This wasn't working for Linc. Every time she kissed him, every time she touched him, Linc compared her to Sonja. Oh, man, was he losing it? No real playa turns down fresh cat! Vera was moving and grinding; she was working herself into an agitated state. Linc's phone began to ring. He had forgotten to turn it to vibrate. Linc was glad he hadn't changed it, he needed an out.

"Give me a minute, this might be important."

The girl moved off Linc's lap back onto the couch where she took his free hand and placed it between her legs. Damn, she was persistent. Linc thought, what the hell? Maybe if I give her a little release, I might be able to get out the front door. So while he talked to his brother, he worked her jewel with his finger. Or should he say, she worked his finger in and out of her spot. Linc finished his call with his brother and hurried her to her completion. He kissed her lightly on the cheek and said he was sorry, but he needed to leave.

Linc got up and left the girl on the couch, still quaking from her release.

♥

Linc was irritated with himself as he walked inside his empty house. He couldn't understand what was happening to him. When Kamrin had called earlier, it was to let Linc know that he was going to be staying a few more days with Tuesdae. He and Tuesdae were going to head over to his house in Gary, Indiana so he could check on his mail. Then they would go to his storage garage and bring back a few more clothes.

Linc was happy that Kamrin wasn't sitting around feeling miserable over Adriane, but he just didn't want him to jump into another relationship too fast.

Linc headed for his office to check his e-mail. He sat at the computer checking out a few sites Nancy had e-mailed him about. Time was getting away from Linc. He had spent over an hour going from site to site, looking at buildings and property jotting down a few notes on the ones he wanted to check out. Linc was in deep thought when his cell phone rang; it was sitting next to his office phone. Linc realized he hadn't checked his office phone for messages. He decided he would check them later. As he reached for the cell phone, Linc noticed the fax that Hunter had sent him on the proposal for the building in Chicago.

Linc grabbed the paper as he answered the phone.

"Hello."

"How fast can you get here?"

"LB?"

"That crazy bitch spotted me and Tuesdae leaving the storage garage and tried to run us off the road."

"I'll see if I can get the next flight out, but why do you need me there?"

"I'm at the police station. They are talking about keeping me, charging me with assault."

"What?"

"After I made sure Tuesdae was fine, I got out of the car and tried to hurt Adriane."

"Damn, man. Did you hit her?"

"No, Tuesdae wouldn't allow me to get my hands around Adriane's neck. That bitch tried to kill us, and Tuesdae saved her."

"Hang tight, LB, I will have Hunter get over there and get you out. I will be there as fast as I can."

"Thanks, big brotha, love you man."

"Love you too."

As soon as Linc got a dial tone, he called Hunter.

Hunter had been out on a date with a little honey he had met earlier that day, when he got the call from Linc. He excused himself and eased out of bed so he could talk to Linc in private.

"How did she know Kamrin was there?"

"I don't know, Hunter, but I'm not going to let my brother sit in jail because she's crazy."

"Don't worry, I got it covered. I will have him out before you even get off the plane."

"Thanks, man. Bye."

Hours later, Linc walked into the police station and right in the middle of a cat fight! Adriane had been there, demanding that the police press charges against Kamrin. But before she could get all of her words out, Tuesdae had her finger straight up in the girl's face. Tuesdae was saying something about snatching her bald and beating her ass Windy City Style! Adriane was pushed against a wall and not looking quite so brave.

It took two officers to hold Tuesdae back. Hunter and Kamrin stepped back and watched this tiny lil' bit talk trash, and everyone in the station was sure she could back it up. Each time she moved her neck and waved her arm, Kamrin knew without a doubt, he had to have this woman, for better or worse.

Linc walked over to his brother. "Damn, man, you didn't need us. That lil' girl got some shit going on all by herself! I think Adriane is going to leave ya ass alone now."

Hunter gave Linc some play as they both watched Kamrin develop a goofy grin on his face. His woman was headed over, so he opened his arms to pull Tuesdae in close.

Tuesdae went in his arm and pressed her head into his strong chest.

"Are you all right, Kam?"

"I'm good, baby; how are you?"

"Fine, let's get out of here." She turned towards Hunter as she spoke.

"Can we leave?"

"Sure, unless you just want to beat her ass for the hell of it."

"Trust me, I thought about it, but I don't want to scare Kam away."

Kamrin smiled down at Tuesdae. "I think you are stuck with me. I could fall hard in love with a woman who would kick some ass for me."

♥

Hunter and Linc stayed the next few days in Kamrin's house while Kamrin and Tuesdae stayed at a hotel. They wanted to make sure Adriane didn't try to trash the place. Once she left the police station, she was mad enough to do just that.

♥

Kamrin and Tuesdae settled themselves into a nice hotel. They had been by each other's side since they met at the restaurant. Kamrin knew his divorce wouldn't be final for a few more weeks, but he was seriously thinking about being with this woman forever.

"Tuesdae, baby, we can still get separate rooms, if you like. I don't want you to think I'm rushing you."

Tuesdae kissed Kamrin and led him over to the bed. Kamrin sat on the bed and pulled her in close between his legs.

"I want to talk to you about Adriane, about the life I shared with her."

"All right, but you don't owe me any explanations. It's clear to me that that woman has to be crazy. If you were mine, I would have never let you go."

"That's something I want you to think about. Adriane and I were married for over five years. I couldn't seem to do anything to make her happy. But she didn't marry me because she wanted me to make her happy. She married me to see how much of my money she could spend. My brother tried to warn me, but I was blinded by her beauty."

"Kamrin, I don't want your money. I learned how to live with what I have and be happy with it. If I'm going to be with someone, dedicate my life to that person, it's not going to be based on how much money he has. It's going to be centered on how he makes me feel, how strong our love is. I want to be with someone who is going to love me, love the children we create. That's what I'm looking for."

Kamrin was so happy. "Tuesdae, I've been looking for you for what seems like a life time." He brought her head in close. Kamrin needed to taste her lips.

"I plan on having you, Kam. Are you sure you're all right with this?"

Kamrin moved her hand over his heart so she could feel just how all right with it he was. Then he moved her hand to his mouth and kissed the palm.

"Yes, I want you, too, baby. I want a lifetime with you. And I want us to have children. I'm not going to rush you into anything. I want you to be sure.

"Thank you, Kam. I feel so blessed to have found you."

"So, do you want separate rooms?"

"No, do you think we can just hold each other?"

"Tuesdae, we can do anything you want."

As Kamrin and Tuesdae held each other, he shared with her the story of his parents. He wanted her to know why he was so willing to give her all the time she needed. Kamrin jumped into his relationship with his first wife and look how that turned out. No, this time it would be different; it even felt different.

♥

Hunter was informed the next day that they had a buyer for Kamrin's house. So, Hunter and Linc made the necessary arrangements for the papers to be signed.

♥

The papers were signed, and Kamrin's house was sold. In less than two weeks, his divorce was going to be final. Finally home, Linc was exhausted. He traveled for a living, but for the last few weeks, it was starting to get a little old. Except for the time he spent visiting his woman. No, she wasn't his. Why did he have to keep reminding himself of that? Linc Stone is a playa for life!

Linc took a shower and slipped on a pair of shorts. First he checked his house phone for messages. He saved the ones he would return and erased all the others. When he finished, Linc headed for his office where he kept his exercise equipment.

After working out for half an hour, Linc walked over to his computer. He was going to check his email when he remembered he hadn't checked the messages on his office phone. The light was flashing bright red; Linc pushed the play button. His body became powerless when he heard her voice. He played the message again.

"Message-Tuesday-10:30 pm. Hi Linc, just wanted to say goodnight."

Sonja had called Tuesday, and now it was Thursday. Linc looked at the clock, it was late. It was too late for him to be calling her on a Thursday night. She had to get up early to get her boys to school. Linc played the message one more time. As he listened to her voice, he felt his partner jump for joy.

Linc had to hold his member down. "Damn, love, just listening to your voice makes my boy jump."

Linc looked at the clock again as he punched Sonja's number. It was close to midnight. The phone rang four times before she picked up. A very groggy voice sounded.

"Hello?"

"Baby?"

"Linc, honey…what's wrong?"

His heart was beating fast, she called him honey. Linc couldn't believe how just the sound of her voice drove him over the edge.

"I miss you, love. Do you miss me?"

Sonja sat up in the bed and pushed away her drowsiness. "Linc, what time is it?"

"It's late. I just got your message. Things have been a little crazy for me lately. I've been back and forth to Chicago trying to work out a deal. My brother, LB, he's going through a divorce, and his wife tried to run him and his girlfriend off the road. And then I had to go to Gary, Indiana because the police were going to arrest him for assault." Linc took a breath. "You didn't answer my question."

"Yes, I do."

"Good!"

He was worn out, and Sonja could hear it in his voice.

"Oh, Linc, you must be tired. I'm sure you need to be sleeping instead of talking on the phone."

"Baby, what I need only you can give me. What are you doing this weekend?"

"Nothing."

"If I send a car for you, will you come to me?"

Sonja was silent. She wanted to be with him, but…it was so hard for Sonja to believe that a man like Linc Stone wanted her.

"Linc, do you think it's a good idea for us to keep seeing one another?"

"Probably not, but I can't seem to help myself. Will you come to me, love?"

Sonja's mind told her to say NO, but her heart took over. "Yes."

"Good! What about the boys?"

"They have plans with their sister this weekend."

"Perfect! In the morning I will call the car rental company. I'll have them deliver a car to you. All you will have to do is put your bags inside and drive. Are you sure you are up for such a long drive? I would come pick you up, but--"

"You don't have to pick me up; I can drive."

"Are you sure, baby?"

"Yes. Once I'm certain Tiffany and the boys are settled, I will get on the road after work."

"I know you have to get up early tomorrow, so I will let you get back to sleep. Sonja?"

"Yes?"

"Thank you, baby. This means a lot to me. Call me before you take off."

Chapter 5

Sonja didn't get much sleep that night. She was too excited about her weekend. After she got the boys off to school, she called Tiffany. She wanted to discuss her plans for the weekend with her daughter.

"So, Tiffany, what do you think?"

"How do you feel about it, Mom? Do you want to go?"

"Yes, I do. Just thinking about spending time with him makes me happy."

"Mommy, I just want you to be happy. And if that fine man makes you happy, well then I say go! You don't have to worry about me and my brothers, I have a full weekend planned for us."

"Why don't you come to the house and stay while I'm gone. At least you won't have to bother with lugging their games back and forth."

"I think I will since Terrell is going to be out of town."

"Thank you, honey. Thanks for letting me talk to you about this."

"You're welcome, Mom. I love you."

"I love you too. I've got to finish getting ready for work. I will see you later."

♥

Later that evening, as Sonja pulled into her driveway, she noticed it. It was the biggest truck she'd ever seen! It looked like a Toyota, and it was the same color as Linc's truck. Tiffany was already at the house waiting on her mother and her brothers. She was looking inside the truck, taking it all in. Matthew and Jeffrey couldn't wait to get inside. They wanted Tiffany to take them for a ride.

Jeffrey pleaded. "Please, Mom, please . Tiffany is a good driver. Can she take us for a ride before you leave?"

"Mom, I can take them to get something to eat while you finish getting ready to go."

Sonja hesitated for just a second. "Fine, but don't be gone long. I want to get on the road soon."

The boys jumped in and buckled up as Tiffany found a rap station on the radio. She had the speakers bumping as she pulled the truck onto the road. Sonja watched her boys as they sat in the back seat, grinning from ear to ear. Sonja thought about just how blessed she was. Her daughter was every mother's dream, and so were her boys. Everyone who met her children seemed to be impressed. They were so well mannered. Tiffany had been a straight A student, as were her boys, and Sonja never had to worry about her children doing something bad, or getting into trouble. Tiffany stayed focused while in school, and Matt and Jeffrey are more interested in playing there Xbox than hanging out on street corners like most boys their age.

She went inside and took a quick shower. Sonja didn't need to pack. She had taken care of that first thing that morning. By the time she was done dressing, Tiffany and her brothers were back. Sonja gave Tiffany Linc's phone number, and she wrote the license plate number of the truck down. Just in case of an emergency. Once she had hugged her boys and her daughter, Sonja waved goodbye and watched Tiffany's car disappear down the road. They were going to Tiffany's to see Terrell before he left town on his business trip.

Sonja went through the house once more making sure to leave the necessary light on for the kids. Just before she walked out the door, she called Linc.

Linc had been driving himself crazy all day waiting for her to arrive. He had gone out and brought new silk sheets for the bed. He bought about five large scented candles for the bathroom, and a few for the kitchen. Linc even picked up scented soap and body wash, and a tube of the same toothpaste he had seen in Sonja's bathroom. He had steaks in the sink covered with seasoning. Linc was going to wait before he put them on his grill. He didn't want them to cook too long; they needed to be just right. The wine was in the freezer chilling. He was tossing the salad when his phone began to ring. Linc looked at the clock, it was almost four p.m.

"Hello."

"Hi, Linc, I'm on my way."

"Good, I had the rental company program my address into the system in the truck. All you have to do is drive. Please be careful. You have my number written down and in your purse, right?"

"Linc, I've driven long distance before; I will be just fine. See you in a few hours."

"Okay, I can't wait to see you, honey. Bye."

Linc turned his cell phone to vibrate, turned the ringer on his office phone off, and the volume on the answering machine all the way down. The ringer on the phone in the living room was off, but the answering machine volume was turned up just a little. When Sonja made it in, he was going to turn that one down, too.

Sonja was enjoying her long ride to Indianapolis, and the weather was splendid for mid-March. Halfway there, she decided to stop at a gas station. She needed to use the restroom. While she was there, she called to check in with her kids. Tiffany informed her that everything was going just fine. Terrell was gone, and she and the boys were on their way to the mall to look around, waste some time, stuff like that. Tiffany told her mother to relax and have a good time. Sonja spoke with her boys before she hung up. Sonja took the gas tank back to full and purchased a bottle of water. Once again, she was on her way.

A few hours later, Sonja pulled in Linc's driveway. Before she could turn the engine off, Linc was standing next to the car door.

"You made it! Come on in. Let me carry your bag." Linc stepped back so Sonja could get out. He got her things out of the backseat and pulled her in close to his frame as he guided her inside his house.

Inside, Linc sat her bag down next to them as he pulled her in for a kiss. As he was kissing Sonja, Linc began removing her things. Sonja pulled away.

"Linc, I'm hungry."

He spoke to her in between kisses. "I'm trying to feed you, baby."

"Stop it," Sonja laughed as she pushed at him. "I smell something wonderful; what is it?"

Linc decided to behave. "I made steaks for us. I have salad and French bread to go along with them, and a bottle of wine."

Linc picked up her bag and gave her a quick kiss. "Let me go put your things in the bedroom, and then we can eat."

As Linc disappeared around the corner, Sonja heard his answering machine click on. The volume was very low, but she could still hear the voice.

"Linc, honey, I'm sorry I missed you. I just wanted to tell you I had a good time the other night. I can't wait to feel you again. Call me soon."

Sonja stood there frozen. What should she do? Should she leave? He never made her any promises, and he wasn't her man. Linc had made that clear from the beginning. She knew that before she agreed to jump in a car and drive for several hours just to make love to him again. Sonja heard Linc coming around the corner, so she turned her back to the machine.

"I hope you are hungry. Come on, love, let's go into the kitchen. I've got everything ready for us."

Sonja was stunned; Linc did have everything ready. The table was set, and he had a vase full of red roses placed in the middle. In various spots of the kitchen, scented candles were placed to help enhance the ambiance.

"Linc, everything looks wonderful. You didn't have to go to so much trouble, not for me."

Linc pulled out her chair for her. As Sonja took her seat, Linc ran his hands over her shoulders.

"If not for you, then who? I just wanted this to be good for you. I want you to feel relaxed, pampered."

Sonja gave him a gentle kiss after taking her seat. While Linc served her, Sonja spoke about her day at work. She told Linc how keyed up the boys and their sister were after seeing the truck he had rented for her. She just knew that by letting Tiffany drive them around in the truck before she left, she was placed way up there in the "coolest mom" category. Linc couldn't believe how much he enjoyed listening to her talk. Didn't matter what she was talking about, everything she said was important to him.

Half hour later, they finished their meal. Linc poured them another glass of wine to take in the living room. He started a fire in the fireplace, and they got comfy on the leather couch. Linc let her get a few drinks of her wine before he overpowered her mouth with ravenous kisses. He was just about to, as they used to say, "get jiggy with it" when he heard the front door opening up.

Linc pulled Sonja under his strong body as he reached for the drawer where he kept one of his guns. Before he removed it all the way, he heard his brother's voice.

"Big brother, where are you, man?" Kamrin came bouncing into the living room. Linc jumped up off the couch and moved away from Sonja. "LB, what the hell are you doing here?"

Kamrin stopped in his tracks when he noticed the good-looking woman sitting on his brother's couch.

"Hi." Kamrin spoke to the woman. Linc was walking towards his brother, almost taking the polish off the wood floors trying to push Kamrin into the other room.

Sonja scarcely got her words out before the two men had disappeared. She wasn't sure what was going on, but she didn't like it, not at all. Linc was acting as if he was ashamed to have her there.

Linc and Kamrin went to Kamrin's bedroom.

"Linc, man, what's going on? How many rules are you breaking? Man, I even left Tuesdae in the car, because you have always been clear on the house rules."

Linc gave his brother a look full of irritation. "LB, why are you here? I thought you and Tuesdae were staying in Chicago?"

"I tried several times to call, but I didn't get an answer. I think you have my wallet, remember? They put all of my things in that envelope at the precinct."

Linc went over to his brother's dresser and opened up the first drawer. The envelope was right there, and inside was Kamrin's wallet. Kamrin took his wallet and looked his brother straight in the eye.

"So, are you turning in your card?"

"What card?"

"Your playas card; your, 'I need more than one woman to satisfy me,' card."

Linc shifted his weight from one side to the other. His brother was starting to get on his nerves with all his questions. "Hell no!"

Kamrin gave his brother a disapproving look before turning and heading out.

"Does she know about your lifestyle?"

"Yes."

"And she's all right with it?"

Linc didn't respond. Kamrin gave his big brother another look as he spoke.

"My woman is waiting for me."

Linc walked out with Kamrin. Kamrin noticed the woman was still sitting on the couch where his big brother had left her. She didn't look happy.

"Goodnight night, Miss. All right, big brother, I will see you in a few days. Later, playa."

Sonja cringed at the other man's words. He had called Linc exactly what he was--a playa. Man, what he must be thinking about her. She was beginning to think that maybe she had made a terrible mistake.

Linc followed LB to the door so he could lock it. He felt like a burglar in his own home as he tip-toed back into the living room. As he entered the room, Linc studied her sweet face; she looked lost.

"I'm going to go clean up the kitchen." Linc waited for her to respond, but she didn't. Sonja wouldn't even look at him.

Sonja sat on the couch concentrating on the fire as she downed her glass of wine, and then she went for Linc's. Sonja's eyes began to get heavy. After she and Linc spoke on the phone the other night, it was hard for her to fall back to sleep. After dragging out of bed the next morning and getting the boys off to school, Sonja scarcely made it through work. It was finally catching up with her. So, she rested her head on the arm of the couch. Before long, she was out.

Linc put the food away and loaded the dishwasher as he wrestled with his feelings. Why had he treated her like she was a stranger? Why didn't he properly introduce Sonja to his brother? He was making a mess of things. He headed back for the living room, only to find Sonja fast asleep on the couch.

Gently he picked Sonja up and carried her to the bedroom, where he removed all of her clothing. Then he removed his and climbed into bed next to her. Linc drew Sonja's warm body in close to his own and waited for his body to allow him to drift off to sleep.

As he laid there so close to her, he thought of all the things he had done all day preparing for her to arrive. Linc looked at the beautiful woman in his arms. He couldn't understand this craving he had for her, but he had to get it under control. It felt as if he had to constantly keep crazy thoughts of love and marriage out of his mind. Linc didn't want to get married. Shit, he didn't want to fall in love and wasn't going to either. Just then, Sonja turned and draped her arms around Linc's neck. She mumbled something and drifted back off to sleep.

Linc moved his hand between their bodies as he touched her soft bud. Sonja gave way a sensual moan and opened up for him.

"Oh, damn." Linc knew he had to have her right then. He moved over her and pushed inside as he whispered in her ear.

"I'm sorry to wake you, baby, but I need you."

Her eyes slowly opened as she felt him enter. The sensation was phenomenal. Sonja sighed as she reached for him. They made love, and then Sonja curled up close to Linc and fell back to sleep. Leaving Linc wondering what the hell was he going to do.

A few hours later, Sonja woke to find Linc sitting on the side of the bed. He was holding his face in his hands.

"Linc, what's wrong?"

Linc wanted to tell her he was getting tired of being controlled by her loving. But she had that raspy thing going on with her voice, and she was running her hand over his back. He turned to look at her. The sheet was around her waist and her breasts were calling out to him.

Linc cursed as he reached for her. Once again, he was riding a wave of passion. This time he was determined to regain control. He was Linc Stone. Women melted from his touch, begged for it. Why should Sonja be any different? So, Linc decided to put his powers to the test. He waited right until she was ready to break, and he pulled out of her heat. If he was right, and he always was when it came to women, Sonja would react like all the other women.

"Linc…what's wrong, honey? Why did you stop?"

"Tell me what you want?" There was a wild look in his eyes.

Sonja didn't miss it. "What are you talking about?"

"Oh come on, Sonja. Let's not pretend; we both know why you are here. Just tell me what you want. Tell me how you want it, and then I want you to beg me to give it to you."

The look on his face was unrecognizable. What was wrong with him?

A confident Linc remained still. "Talk to me, Sonja."

For the fist time in many years, Sonja thought briefly about her first husband. The way he needed to use and control her, how it made him feel like a big man. Sonja vowed a long time ago to never put herself in a position like that again. It took her years to believe in herself again, regain her self-esteem. She tossed her bad memories back down where they belonged and began to build her wall of protection.

"Linc, get off of me!"

"What?" That wasn't the answer he was used to.

"Get off of me, Linc. Now!" Sonja gave him a push.

Seconds later, it became crystal clear to Linc. He'd made a terrible mistake. Linc wished his words could be taken back, but that was impossible with his foot in his mouth. The damage was done, and he didn't know how to correct.

"Baby, wait." Linc began to move trying to regain some of the passion that they generally shared.

Sonja's body betrayed her. With tears streaming down her face, she aided him in bringing them to completion. Once their satisfaction was obtained, Sonja pushed Linc off of her, and she got out of bed. Linc watched as she went around the room looking for her clothes.

"Sonja, what are you doing?"

She wouldn't answer. Sonja continued with her search.

"Baby, please stop."

Sonja whirled on him fast. "Stop what? Stop letting you treat me like I'm one of your young, silly, sex driven females. Stop allowing your behavior towards me to teach my boys that's it's all right to treat a woman like she's a piece of property. Hey, if it's good enough for their mother…"

"I'm not treating you like that."

"Oh no, I forgot! I'm just a booty call."

"Baby, stop it. I don't know why I said those things; come back to bed."

Sonja was angry. She was hurt, and it was clear in her appearance and her dialogue. She continued searching for her things.

"No, thank you, I've had enough to last me a lifetime. First you bring me to your home where I have to listen to a call from one of your women. Oh, you must have put it on her good, she cant wait until the two of you get back together so she can have some more! Then your brother stopped by, and all of a sudden, I must have rabies. You practically jumped five feet away from me when he came into the room.

And now you want me to beg you for sex? I've already visited hell, a special trip given to me by my first husband, and I'm not going back."

Linc couldn't speak. Even if he could, he knew she wouldn't listen.

"Where is my bag?"

"The bag is in the closet...but..."

She went to the closet and found the carryon bag sitting on the floor. It was empty. Linc had cleared out half of a dresser drawer for her things.

"Where are my things?"

Linc couldn't answer; he was having a hard time just trying to look at her. He had hurt her. It was killing him, but he had no idea what he had just done to her soul.

Sonja shoved the empty bag under her arm and headed for the door. "Forget it. I just want to get out of here."

Linc looked at the clock. It wasn't quite four in the morning.

"Sonja, you can't leave now, wait a few more hours so you can have more daylight."

She kept right on walking. Linc knew if he tried to move, his legs would give out on him. He had really messed up this time. Somehow, Linc knew he had lost her. Linc sat on the side of the bed as part of the sheet covered his body. He listened to the front door close.

♥

After what seemed like hours, Linc finally was able to move from the bed. He grabbed a pair of pajama bottoms and pulled them on as he made his way to the living room. He pushed the button on the answering machine and listened to his messages. He heard the message Sonja had referred to. He also heard Kamrin's voice on the machine. There were a few more calls from women, and there was a hang up.

♥

This was Sonja's third time pulling over out of the flow of traffic, because she couldn't control her tears. But this time she noticed bright lights flashing behind her. Sonja watched through her tears as the officer approached the truck.

Mario Rios shift was almost over and he was ready to get home to his wife. Mario got out of his marked police car and headed for the vehicle he had just stopped. He had noticed her because her truck kept swerving into the other lines. Lightly he tapped on the driver side window and noticed right away the woman behind the wheel was crying.

"Miss, is there a problem?"

"I'm sorry officer." Sonja began to cry once more.

The officer, aware of the steady flow of traffic buzzing by him, decided this was not the place to speak to this woman. Something was wrong. It was his duty to help her, if he could. This woman needed help not a ticket.

"Miss, I'm going to need you to go to the next exit and pull into the truck stop."

Feeling no need to fear the officer, Sonja pushed her tears aside and did what the officer asked. Officer Rios followed Sonja and instructed her to go inside. They were going to have a cup of coffee. He needed to reassure himself that she was going to be fine. Sitting across the table from her, the officer studied her for a moment. He found her to be very attractive. She reminded him of his own wife. The wife he was tying to get home to.

Mario gave Sonja a bright smile. "Miss, this is the end of my shift, and I'm anxious to get home to my wife, but I want to help you if I can,. . So, why don't you tell me what's so bad that you have to pull over and cry?"

Sonja felt so stupid. "I think I just broke up with my boyfriend, but he was never really mine."

Mario smiled. What the woman said didn't make since, but it did! "Well, I can honestly say that it's his loss."

Sonja forced a smile at the nice man. "Thank you…"

"It's Mario."

"Thank you, Mario. I'm Sonja."

As Mario was greeting her with a hand shake, a call came through on his radio.

"Okay, Sonja. I've got to go. Looks like you and I just missed an accident right down the road. I want you to finish your coffee before you get back behind the wheel of your car."

"Thank you, Mario. If you hadn't come along, I might have been a part of that accident. You were my guardian angel." She said a silent prayer for those who weren't as fortunate.

"Enjoy the rest of your weekend, Sonja."

♥

Linc sat down on the couch and watched the door, but he knew she wasn't coming back. Linc kept looking at the clock. He wanted to call Sonja, but he needed to give her time to get home. Linc wasn't sure what he was going to say.

♥

Sonja decided to take her time. She didn't want to go home and have to answer a bunch of questions from her family. As day light approached and businesses were opening, she stopped, went into a few stores to pick up a couple of things for her children.

Chapter 6

It was after eight in the morning, and Linc was still sitting on the couch looking into the fireplace. The fire had burned out long ago. He heard someone knocking at the door, but he couldn't get up. Why should he? He knew when he opened it, the person standing there wasn't going to be Sonja.

Hunter walked in the living room and stopped when he found his friend sitting on the couch.

"Linc, man, where were you this morning? Did you forget about the phone conference we had scheduled?"

Linc finally looked away from the fireplace. What Hunter saw alarmed him.

"Linc, what the hell is going on here? What happened to you?"

"I fucked up! I lost her, man. She's never gonna take me back, not after the way I treated her. Every time I close my eyes, I can see that look of horror on her beautiful face."

"Whoa, whoa, whoa! What are you talking about? Or should I say who? You are Linc Stone; you don't deal with just one woman. Do you?"

"No, I don't. Well I didn't, but then I met her. Hunter, this woman is special, different. It's funny. Everything I swore I would never have, nor would I want in my life, she represents it. But when I held her in my arms that New Year's night, I knew my life was going to change. No matter how hard I've fought it, I can't deny that I have feelings for this woman. She is the first woman that's made me even envision the possibility of slowing down, and now I've pushed her away. I let my stupid pride get in the way. I was so worried about my playa-status that I was afraid to show her how I felt. I've lost her."

It took Hunter a few moments to collect his thoughts. For what seemed like the first time in many years, Hunter Merrill, a successful lawyer, was at a loss for words. He studied his friend for a few more moments, allowing what Linc had said to sink in. At first, Hunter found this whole scenario to be unbelievable. The more he thought about it, he said to himself, "Why not?" For as much as Linc wanted to deny it, even he needed a special someone in his life. Quiet as it's kept, Hunter could foresee the same thing happening for him somewhere in the future.

"Okay, I don't know who you are talking about, but it's obvious this woman means a lot to you. It's clear she is supposed to be in your life, or it wouldn't be affecting you this way. Man, let me hip you to something. You don't have to be a playa for the rest of your life. You've had your share of women. Leave some for the rest of us! Beside, happiness doesn't always find everyone, and if you think you have found it, don't let it slip away."

"She was so mad when she left here. I've been sitting here waiting, trying to give her enough time to calm down, to get back home safe. I want to call her, try to talk to her. Do you think I should call her today?"

"Well knowing you, I'm sure you won't rest until you know she's safe. But, when you call her, try to keep it short. If she's still upset, you don't want to add any more to it. I wouldn't try to make her talk about whatever it was that went down here. You have got to give her time to calm down."

Hunter wanted to smile, but didn't. Hunter never thought he would see the day when Linc Stone was allowing another man to give him advice on women. Hunter couldn't wait to meet the woman that had his friend all shook up. She must be some kind of woman to have blown Linc's mind.

Hunter gave Linc a reassuring pat on the back before the two headed for the front door.

"Thanks, man. At least I don't have to worry about anything else going crazy in my life. LB is all taken care of. You, you never seem to have any problems. Now all I have to do is concentrate on getting my baby back."

"That's cool, man. Look, if you want, I can take care of those calls by myself."

"Thanks, man; I owe you."

"Go fix yourself some coffee, take a shower. Try to relax so you will be calm when you call her. I will check in on you in a few days, unless you need me before then. You know I got your back."

Hunter left, and Linc went to start his coffee and prepare for his shower.

♥

Sonja felt as if the ride home had taken a lifetime. She took her packages out of the truck and headed inside her house. The kids weren't home, so Sonja decided to place a call to the car rental company. After being transferred around for fifteen minutes, they informed her that Mr. Stone had to request them to pick up the car. Then they could see about giving him a refund on the days the car wasn't used. When Sonja asked if someone there could call Linc, the person on the other end of the line began to laugh as if Sonja had just cracked a joke. No, the sales person finally told her; Linc would have to call them. Sonja didn't find any humor in the situation. She decided not to take the matter any future and hung up the phone. Sonja wasn't happy. Sonja took in a deep breath, it was then she realized she could still smell Linc. His magnetic scent was all over her body. Sonja brushed away a stray tear as she headed for the shower. Before she could get too far, her phone rang.

"Hello."

Linc could hear her fatigue. He reminded himself not to push her. "Hey, love."

Sonja's pulse quickened at the smooth sound of his voice. That made her angry. She didn't want to want him, miss him, to look at his handsome face.

"Don't call me that. When a person uses words of endearment, there is usually some kind of feelings that go with them."

Linc was silent. There were feelings behind his words, he just didn't know how to convey them.

"What do you want, Linc?"

"I just wanted to make sure you made it home safe."

"Yes, I did. You need to call the car rental company and tell them to come and pick up their truck. They said you had to be the one to request the pick up."

"Why don't you use the truck until Monday?"

"No. Call them."

Frustrated with the situation, Linc wondered why he was putting himself through this. Then he remembered Sonja's face, her smell, her touch, her taste, and vowed to take his scolding and do whatever it took to get her back.

"Baby, why don't you let the kids us it. I'm sure Tiffany and Terrell would enjoy riding around in it, and so would Matthew and Jeffrey."

"Fine, I need to take a shower and lay down. I have to go."

"Baby, I…"

She could hear the hurt in his voice, and Sonja couldn't take it. But she had to be strong, or she would be right back in that truck headed for Indianapolis and back in his bed.

Sonja had to end the call. She could feel her brick wall, her fortress, starting to crumble. Her words came out soft but full of pain. "Linc, please don't. I can't cry anymore. Goodbye."

Linc listened to the dial tone until that little voice came through "If you would like to make a call…" He hung up. This time when he got a drink, it wasn't coffee; he got himself a shot of whiskey.

♥

Later that evening when Tiffany and her brothers arrived home, they found their mother sitting in the living room waiting for them.

Tiffany hugged her mom "Mom, what are you doing here? I thought we wouldn't see you until tomorrow."

Tiffany waited for her brothers to let their mom come up for air. They were happy to see her.

"I started missing my children, so I cut my plans short. Here I am! Boys, why don't you go get your game box and bring it out; we can play for a while."

As soon as Matthew and Jeffrey were out of ear shot, Tiffany asked her mother again.

"Okay, spill it."

"Oh, Tiffany, I think your mom is destined to be single. I should have known from the start that he was way out of my league."

"Mommy, you've always taught us to believe that there isn't anything out of our reach, if we really and truly want it. The question is, do you really and truly want a future with Linc."

Matthew and Jeffrey were racing back into the room with their game. They were ready to play.

She didn't get a chance to answer Tiffany, but that was cool. She needed time to think about the answer to that question.

After Sonja played a few games with Matthew and Jeffrey, she informed Tiffany that Linc said she could take the truck home with her. She just needed to have it back by Monday morning. Tiffany was excited, and so were the boys. Before Tiffany left, she took her brothers for a nice long ride.

Later on that night, Sonja laid in bed fighting off the urge to call Linc. She wanted to hear his voice. But, after a few hours of tossing and turning, she realized something. If Linc really wanted her, he would have called back, tried to make things right. But Sonja knew a man like Linc Stone would never want to be with a woman like her. A man like him didn't have just one woman. But in order to be with him, she would have to share him. Sonja didn't want to share him; she wanted him in a way she knew she couldn't have him. Linc Stone was a ladies' man. It was clear that they had made a huge mistake. They should have stopped after that one night. After all, that's all he had promised her. Now look at the mess they created.

♥

Connie looked over at her son. Every time she looked at the slight bruise on his face her heart hurt. And it also reminded her of the bruises she was sporting. Connie's husband was the reason she and her son had those nice shiners. It seemed that for over a year now, Connie was becoming increasingly fearful for the life of her thirteen year old son.

About six years ago when Connie met her husband, she thought it would only be a matter of time before he fell in love with her son. Why wouldn't he? Her son was very well mannered, and as cute as can be! But a few months after they married, she began noticing her son's behavior. Lincoln was never a very talkative person, but whenever his step-father was around, the boy never said a word.

Things got worse when Connie became pregnant. When their daughter was born, her husband started acting as if the sight of Lincoln made him sick. Connie feared what might happen to her son if he were left alone with his step-father. So for five years, Connie kept her son close by. Her husband began to make comments about that, too. He felt as if Lincoln was taking up far too much of Connie's time. Her husband, Kim, had had enough, and he began to act out on his feelings. It started with a few ugly comments to Lincoln when he thought Connie couldn't hear him, and it just escalated from there.

When their daughter, Kimberly, became old enough to participate in activities outside of the house, Connie was forced at times to leave Lincoln home alone, or worse, with his step-father. Kim had begun to change his step-son. No longer was he that quiet child. No, Lincoln had too much of his father in him. He began to rebel. Lincoln had never seen his father, but Connie had always talked to him about his father. Connie told her son that he was from a long line of strong men.

Connie looked over at her son once more. She ran a shaky hand over his soft curly hair. The boy looked over at his mom and tried to smile.

"Mom, I'm getting hungry. When can we stop?"

"Baby, do you think you can hold out for a few more minutes? We are almost to your father's house."

They had been riding for hours, but Connie was still too afraid to stop. She didn't think Kim had followed them, but she wasn't confident or brave enough to find out.

"Okay."

Connie reached inside her purse and pulled out a candy bar; she handed it to her son. He showed her his father's smile before he devoured the Snickers bar.

As she drove down the highway, the ugly events of the evening haunted her. Hours earlier, Connie and her husband were in the middle of their umpteenth fight. Lincoln had left his shoes on the stairs, and Kim was upset that he had to look at them. Kim's stance had always been, wasn't it enough that he had to take care of another man's son? Why did he have to pick up after him, too?

Connie could still hear Kim screaming at her son. *"Lincoln! Come here and get these dirty shoes off my steps!"*

Connie knew her son. Over the years he had learned that if he just did what his step-father asked of him, it still wasn't enough. So for his own sanity, the young boy learned to block his step-father out. And that set Kim on fire!

Tired of just the sound of the man's voice, slowly Lincoln walked over to the steps to pick up the shoes to take them to his minuscule room. As he bent down to pick them up, Kim pushed the boy over. Lincoln had grown tired of all of this. He was only thirteen years old. Although he loved his mother, his step-dad was really asking for it. Lincoln was trying to get up when Kim punched the boy in the face. Connie was on her way down the stairs when she saw her husband hit her son. Connie hadn't wanted this day to come, but here it was. Well, Lincoln had been pushed too far.

Connie screamed as she charged down the stairs at them. But Lincoln was too much like his father. He struck his step-dad where it really hurt. The blow sent Kim sailing backwards, and he lost his balance. Connie was just as surprised as Kim by her son's actions. She made sure her son was fine, and then she went to the aide of her husband. Kim was so mad he hit Connie across her face and told her to get her bastard son out of his house.

Connie had to gently grab a hold of her son, because he was going after his step-father again for hitting his mom. She tenderly guided him up the stairs and into his room. She instructed him to pack what he could and leave the rest. Connie went into the boy's closet and reached on to top shelf for a small box. Inside the box was an envelope, containing all of Lincoln's important papers.

As they made their way back down the stairs, Kim was waiting for them. He told Connie to take the boy to her parents or else she had to take him to a boy's camp; he was no longer welcome in his house. And if she tried to bring Lincoln back, he would divorce her and take Kimberly far away. She would never see her daughter again.

Connie thought about going to her in-laws, but she decided against it. She thought that if she could just get her son to safety, all would be well. Connie cared deeply for her in-laws, as they did her, so she didn't want to put them in the middle. At first, his family wasn't too happy with his decision to marry Connie. Once they met her, they fell in love with her. His parents took to Lincoln also. Kim didn't like that at all. It was as if his marrying Connie was his way of rebelling. He soon found out that his plan had backfired, and now his true colors were shining through.

So, Connie was taking her son to the one place she knew he would be safe.

♥

Linc was on his third drink when someone knocked on his front door. He didn't get up. But it seemed the person at the door wasn't getting it; they weren't going to leave. Finally, the knocking had started to piss him off. Linc stormed to the door and snatched it open. Disbelief and shock registered on his face as he looked at the person standing in front of him. How the hell had she found him, and why?

"Connie? What the hell? How did you find me?"

Linc stared at Connie in disbelief; he hadn't seen her in years. The last time they were together, she had been fighting with her boyfriend and wanted Linc to comfort her. That had been well over thirteen years. Now she was standing on his doorstep. Linc noticed that she was wearing sunglasses, but it was late in the evening.

"Linc, can I come in?"

Linc stepped back to give her room to enter. Before she did, she turned to her car and motioned for the person inside to come join her. A few seconds later, a young man was standing by Connie's side. His pants were just above the top of his shoes; his coat looked like it was from a rummage sale, and his tee-shirt was tight. He was carrying two bags. For a split second, Linc could see his father in the young man's face!

"Connie, what is going on here?"

"Linc, let me introduce you to your son, Lincoln Stone Jr. Lincoln, honey, say hello to your father."

A developing baritone voice came out strong. "Hello, Dad."

Linc was astonished. "Hi." Linc pulled Connie to the side. "Connie, how old is he?"

"He's thirteen. Isn't he beautiful?"

"Yes, he is very handsome. Connie, if he is mine—"

"Linc, he is yours. Just look at him."

"Why didn't you tell me? Why are you here now?"

"He is at the age where he needs his father. Please take him."

"What? Take him? Where are you going? Take him for how long?"

Connie turned towards her son. "Lincoln, honey, go over and look at those pictures that are sitting on the mantel over the fireplace? They are pictures of your grandfather and your uncle Kamrin."

The boy walked over so his mom and his newly found father could talk.

"Linc, things at home are not good. I need to make sure Lincoln is going to be taken care of. I think it would make him happy to be with his father."

"Connie, are you in trouble?"

"Nothing I can't handle, as long as I know you are taking care of our son. Please, Linc, let him stay."

"Connie I don't even know him. He doesn't know me. Besides, I don't have room in my life for a child. He will only get in the way."

"Linc, he needs you. Look at him and tell me you could turn your back on your own child."

"Connie, why would you keep something like this from me? How have you been able to take care of him?"

"I'm a survivor! Besides, if I had told you I was pregnant, you would not have rested until I had an abortion. And then we would have hated ourselves, and each other, for the rest of our lives."

Linc looked over at the young man. "Connie, you should have told me. I don't understand. You always took birth control."

"If you remember, Bruce and I were having a few problems when I ran into you. We had decided that we wanted a child, but I couldn't get pregnant. Well, we went to see my doctor, and that's when everything went sour. Bruce found out that we couldn't get pregnant, but not because of me, it was because of him. Bruce wouldn't accept it. He swore I had done something crazy, like paid the doctor to say that it was him and not me. Because there couldn't be anything wrong with him. He left me and never looked back."

Linc shock his head. "He was your choice, just remember that."

Linc's harsh words made Connie cringe. She had picked Bruce over Linc, because she thought he could give her a better life.

"Sorry, that was an ugly thing to say. But thirteen years Connie? I'm…I'm sorry I wasn't there for you." He looked once more at the young boy standing admiring the photos.

"But you are here for our son now, right?"

Linc's mind was whirling. Man, he had a son. What was happening to his life? He couldn't have a son. Linc began to pace back and forth. First this thing with Sonja, and now he finds out he has a son. He can't turn his back on his son. His father would turn over in his grave if he did. Linc looked at Connie and gave her a reluctant nod.

Connie released the air she had pent up inside. "Lincoln, honey, come give Mom a kiss goodbye. You are going to be okay here. Your father is going to take great care of you. After all, you are just like him. You are both strong men."

Lincoln went to his mother. "Momma, what about you; you're not going back there, are you?"

Connie talked close to her son's ear. "Honey, your sister is still there. He won't let me leave there with her, and I won't leave her there. As soon as he calms down, I will call you, check on you. See how good you and your dad are getting along."

Lincoln held his mother tight as she kissed him on the forehead and told him again just how much she loved him. With tears streaming, she headed for the door.

Linc was fast behind her. "Wait, Connie, for how long?"

Connie handed Linc an envelope and turned and almost ran out the door.

Linc and his son stood and just looked at one another for a moment. Finally, Linc spoke.

"Well, Lincoln, let me show you to your room." It was then that Linc noticed the bruise on his son's face.

"Who hit you?"

"My step-dad."

Linc's chest tightened. "Is that why your mom brought you here?"

"Yeah, she thought he was going to try and really hurt me. I'll bet he's re-thinking that. When he hit me, I hit him back. That's when he hit Mom. She tried to jump between us, so he hit her. He told her I wasn't welcome in his house, and if she tried to bring me back, he was going to put me out on the streets or something."

"What?"

"My mom is really frightened. She thinks he is going to take my little sister from her."

"What's this fool's name?"

"Kim Vance."

"Kim? I've never met a brotha named Kim."

"He's not a brotha; he's white."

"What? Connie married a white man?"

"Yeah, why?"

"Nothing, I just can't imagine Connie... Well, maybe. Don't get me wrong, there's nothing wrong with it. I'm just a little surprised."

Linc showed Lincoln around the house and then fixed him something to eat. Linc knew Lincoln was hungry when he heard the boy's stomach growl so loud he thought a lion was in the room.

Linc helped the boy get settled. After he ate and had a bath, it didn't take him long to fall fast asleep. That's when Linc called his brother.

"LB, man, I hope you are still in town. I need you to get here as fast as you can."

Kamrin didn't ask any questions. He told his brother he was on his way. Within twenty minutes, Kamrin and Tuesdae were in the driveway.

Kamrin entered the house to find his brother waiting by the door.

Linc looked behind Kamrin. "Where is your woman?"

"She's in the car."

"Get her, man; she is welcome in our home."

Kamrin gave his brother one second to change his mind, and then went to the door and motioned for Tuesdae to come inside. Once she was in, Kamrin asked his brother what was going on.

"LB, you had better sit down."

"Man, you are scaring me. Just tell me what it is."

Instead of talking, Linc motioned for his brother and Tuesdae to follow him. They stopped in front of the extra bedroom. Linc remained silent as they slowly entered the room, careful not to disturb the occupant. Kamrin couldn't believe what he was seeing. The three stood there amazed at the little person fast asleep in the bed.

"Linc, what the hell, man?"

"That's your nephew. His name is Lincoln Stone Jr. Connie is his mother. All those years, and she never told me."

Kamrin was still in shock. "Congratulations, man. I'm an uncle. Wow, I need a drink, man!"

Tuesdae smiled at the two men as they embraced. She wanted to give them some privacy.

Leisurely touching Kamrin's arm, she spoke. "If you can show me where the kitchen is, I will make us some coffee."

Kamrin took Tuesdae to the kitchen and showed her where everything was located before he joined his brother in the living room.

"LB, what I'm I going to do?"

"You are going to be the best damn father that little boy ever dreamed he would have."

"What if I can't do it? What if I let him down, like Mom let us down?"

"Linc, man, you are nothing like Mom. You are more like Dad than either of us. You are the strong one. You are the one who takes care of me and anyone else that needs it. Just look at how you were prepared for Adriane. I would have never done any of the things you did. If anyone is like Mom, it's me. Sometimes I feel so needy. I think that was her problem. She needed so much, but she never realized she had everything she would ever need."

"But don't...don't you think Dad lived a life of hell?"

"Man, Dad loved us, and he loved Mom. Seeing our ugly faces made his day. He made a choice, and it was us. I don't think he had any regrets. Have you ever thought how strong a person would have to be to put up with the shit Daddy did? That was one strong man, just like you are."

Linc was still holding onto the envelope Connie had handed to him. Slowly he opened it up. Inside was Lincoln's birth certificate. Linc noticed his name was printed in the spot marked, FATHER. Young Lincoln's shot record and dental records were there also. There was also a transcript from his school, along with his social security card.

"Man, look at me. I've been thrown off balance. This isn't right. I'm Linc Stone. I'm a playa; a hard working man who never wanted anything more than a good deal and a different honey every other week."

Kamrin smiled at his brother. "So Linc, what are you going to do?"

"First thing in the morning I'm going to call Hunter. I will have him get started with custody papers. What else can I do?"

"Will Connie sign?"

"I'm not going to give her an option. I won't let my boy go back to that place. He told me his step-father hit him; he even hit Connie."

"Hell no! Who is this fool?"

"Not sure, but I plan on knowing everything there is to know about him. And then I'm going to invite him to put his hands on me."

Kamrin nodded. He knew his brother was going to do exactly what he said. He planned on being right by his side when he did.

Chapter 7

The next morning, bright and early, Linc called Hunter and asked him to come out to the house.

"I got here as soon as I could, what's up?" Hunter asked.

Linc walked Hunter into the kitchen. Lincoln was sitting at the table finishing his breakfast.

"Lincoln, wipe off your hands and come say hello to your Uncle Hunter."

"Hello, Uncle Hunter. Dad, I thought Uncle Kamrin was your only brother?"

"LB is my blood brother, but Hunter here, he's my brotha! You feel me?"

Lincoln smiled at his father. "Yes, sir, I feel ya!"

"Okay, little man, finish your meal, and then go take your bath."

"It was nice to meet you Uncle Hunter."

"Same here, Lincoln!"

Hunter watched Linc with the young boy. Hunter couldn't believe his own eyes. Linc was a different man. The Linc Stone Hunter had become friends with was not this man. No, the man Hunter once knew would not have opened his arms to the young Linc. The old Linc Stone would have told Connie he had nothing for her and closed the door. Hunter was pleased and amazed with the new Linc. Somehow, Hunter knew Linc's lady friend had a lot to do with the new Linc. He waited for the boy to disappear around the corner before he started.

"Man, what is going on?"

"Hunter, my whole life has been turned upside down."

"How old is he, man?"

"Thirteen! I need you to put everything else on hold. We need to find out everything there is to know about this step-dad of his. I didn't tell you the best part. The fool hit my boy, and his mother, Connie."

Hunter just shook his head. He had known Linc for a long time. The first thing he had learned right away was that you don't mess with Linc's loved ones. The shit was about to be on.

♥

First thing Monday morning, Linc and Hunter obtained temporary custody papers until Connie could be served with permanent custody forms. Then they enrolled Lincoln into a private school in Indianapolis. Lincoln wouldn't be able to start until the following Monday.

After they were through with all the formalities, Linc, Hunter and Kamrin took the young Lincoln shopping. When they returned, they were met at Linc's door by Tuesdae. She arrived bearing gifts for young Lincoln. For the rest of the night, Lincoln was entertained with board games and a Game Boy, along with some educational books for him to read. Linc was feeling good. He never knew having a child could make him feel so good. Everything was in place, except he needed his woman. Sonja was still on Linc's mind.

Later that night, when Linc went in his son's room to check on him, young Linc was wide wake, and he wanted to talk.

"Dad, do you think Mom is all right?"

Linc was still so surprised that the boy didn't hesitate to call him Dad. How quickly he found comfort in his father's home and his arms. Linc could feel his heart beating, filling up with love for his son. For so many years, Linc had trained his heart to operate like stone. Then he met Sonja, and he could feel his heart start to soften, no matter how hard he fought it. And then life played a crazy trick on him; he found out he was someone's father. As ridiculous as it might sound to anyone who knew him, he was enjoying it.

"I can only hope so. I've got Uncle Hunter looking into some things for me concerning your step-dad. I'm going to do my best to help your mom out of this mess."

"I miss her. I hope I can see her soon."

"Lincoln, I never asked you how you felt about me retaining permanent custody of you. How do you feel?"

"I think it's cool! I've dreamt of being with you for so long. I'm just worried about my mom."

"You're not worried about your little sister?"

"Naw, he would never lay a finger on Kimberly."

"How do you feel about her?"

Lincoln thought for a moment about his baby sister. "I love her! She's cool. We get along great. I miss her too, but she's not the one in danger."

"I know it's easy to say don't worry. But I don't want you to focus too much on this situation with your mom. Let me take care of it for you. All I expect you to do is have fun being young."

"You are just the way I imagined you would be. Mom always told me when the time came for you to step in, you would, and everything would be fine. She was right."

Linc was caught off guard when young Lincoln reached up and pulled his father in for a tight hug. Linc was feeling good. He never knew fatherhood could feel so good. The only other time he ever felt complete was when he held Sonja in his arms.

♥

Weeks had gone by. Linc, Kamrin and Hunter were very busy. Hunter had found out quite a bit about Mr. Kim Vance. He came from money, but he himself didn't necessarily have any, only what his parents gave him. He had a job in the family business where he did absolutely nothing but collect a pay check.

♥

Tiffany called her mother at work. It was Friday, and she wanted to give her mom a break. She and Terrell were going to pick the boys up from school, take them to a movie, and out to eat. Tiffany told her mother to plan on relaxing for the weekend.

Sonja had just pulled into her driveway when she heard Dexter calling out to her. He was jogging towards her from his yard; he looked so serious.

"Hey, Dex, what's wrong?"

"Sonja, I'm glad I caught you. Listen, I need a big favor from you. Remember last year when my co-worker from Arizona came to town to help me with training?"

"Yes, nice looking man. What was his name again? Ty wasn't it?"

"Good, you do remember him. Look, Jenna and I want to go out to dinner and maybe a movie, but her friend cancelled on Ty at the last minute. I think she's coming down with the flu or something. Please, please say you will fill in for her."

"Dex, I'm not sure I would be good company."

"Come on, Sonja. He requested you. It seems you made a lasting impression on him his previous trip. Just dinner and a movie, I promise."

She thought about it for a minute. Why should she stay home and continue to sulk?

"Okay, what time are we leaving?"

"Thank you, Sonja! I will send Ty over about five-thirty, if that's cool."

"Fine, I will be waiting for him at the door."

♥

Linc had just finished saying goodbye to his son. Lincoln was going to hang out with his Uncle Kamrin and Tuesdae for the weekend. Linc was going to make a run to Dowagiac. He figured he had given Sonja enough time to cool down. More than enough. With everything going on lately, Linc had so much to share with her. He couldn't wait to put his arms around her and kiss her soundly.

By the time he got on the road, it was almost noon. Maybe he would catch her and the boys at dinnertime. Maybe he would get real lucky and her daughter and son-in-law would have the boys for the weekend.

♥

Sonja took a shower and changed into a nice pair of jeans and a light sweater. After she re-applied her make-up, Sonja noticed she was running a little behind schedule, so she grabbed her purse and headed for the front door.

Linc was pulling into Sonja's driveway when he noticed the man standing outside the front door.

Just as Sonja was opening the door, Ty rang the door bell.

Ty Shivers was a mouth-watering man in his late thirties. He had to stand six foot three at least. Although he kept his hair cut short, it looked like fine silk, and it was midnight black. His skin was the color of sweet caramel, and his physique was hands down one of the best Sonja had ever laid eyes on. But he wasn't Linc Stone. No matter how she might try, no other man could ever compare to Linc.

"Sonja! You look delicious!" Ty said with a smile.

Sonja had stepped outside and was attempting to lock her front door when she heard the other voice.

"She is delicious, and she belongs to me," Linc stated.

Sonja slowly turned to find Linc and Ty facing one another, eye to eye. Neither one budged. Was Ty crazy? Linc looked as if he was going to rip his head off.

Ty moved his large frame in front of her. "Sonja, do you know this man?"

Linc reach around Ty and tried to pull Sonja into his arms. Sonja pulled away from him. She knew if he started touching her, she would lose control from just his touch.

"Linc, what are you doing here?"

Linc remained focused on the man Sonja was standing by.

Ty pulled Sonja in a little too close for Linc's liking.

"Linc, I asked you a question."

"I came to see you; we need to talk."

Ty wasn't going to give her up without a fight.

"Sonja, we need to get going if we plan on eating before the movie. It starts in two hours."

"Ty, please give me just a minute."

Ty slowly walked away. Sonja was his date. He didn't want to leave her, but he didn't want to upset Sonja by fighting this man.

"Linc, I don't have time to talk right now. I'm on my way out."

"Sonja, what's going on here? Who is that guy? I don't like the way he's touching you."

Sonja gave him a look. "You don't like… Linc, I have to go."

"Sonja, don't walk away from me. I've come along way to talk with you. I need to talk to you, baby, please."

Sonja slowed her steps. She turned to look at the man she desired more than any other man, but then she remembered the last time they were together. She remembered Linc giving her a glimpse of who he really was. Linc Stone was, and will always be, a playa! Sonja turned and walked away. She didn't look back.

Linc watched her walk away. He was fuming. Just who was that man? If Sonja thought he was just going to let her go, she could forget it. Sonja was his! Linc thought about following them, but he decided that wasn't a good idea. Instead, he got back in his ride. He decided to get something to eat and do a little shopping for his son. When Sonja returned, he would be right here waiting for her.

Dexter and Jenna were sitting in the car, while Ty stood holding the car door open for Sonja. Yes, he had walked away when Sonja asked him to, but when he reached Dex's car, Ty never took his eyes off of Sonja.

"Are you sure everything is fine, Sonja?"

"Yes, Ty, but thank you for asking."

Sonja smiled at the very good looking man before she got inside the car. Within seconds, Ty was sitting very close to her in the backseat.

The two couples shared dinner and conversation before taking in a movie. After the movie, they went for coffee. It was almost 10 pm when Dexter pulled into his driveway. Dexter and Jenna went inside, and Ty walked Sonja to her front door.

Linc was parked down the street from Sonja's house. His blood started to cook as he watched Sonja and that man walk to her front door. The man was still touching and feeling all over Sonja, and Linc didn't like it, not at all. Linc made himself sit in the car and wait for the dude to leave.

Ty asked if he could come inside for a while, he wanted to give Dex and Jenna some time alone. Sonja decided it wouldn't hurt, so she invited him inside. She turned the living room light on and told Ty to have a seat. They watched a little television and just talked. Sonja really liked Ty. He was fine, smart, and easy to get along with. She had a really good time with him tonight.

After about an hour, Ty decided he had given Dexter and his woman more than enough time. He asked if he could exit through the back door. That way, he could enter Dex's house from the back, and hopefully, not disturb Dex and Jenna.

Sonja walked Ty to the back door and allowed him to quickly kiss her goodnight. Ty was all right with that, he could wait. He had known from the first time he met her over a year ago that she would be worth the wait. She had just lost her husband, and he didn't want to push her.

Once Ty was out the back door, Sonja went into the living room, turned out the light, and headed for her bedroom to undress.

Linc was still watching Sonja's house. He never saw the man leave, but she was turning off all the lights. "What the hell?" Linc jumped out of the car and headed for Sonja's front door.

Sonja had just finished undressing and was getting ready to pull her nightgown out of the drawer when she heard someone ringing her doorbell and knocking on her front door. She wasn't sure what was going on, so she grabbed her robe and ran to see who it was.

She heard him through the door. It was Linc.

"Baby, I know you're in there; open the damn door!"

Sonja pulled the door open, and before she could move out of his way, Linc lifted her up off the floor and moved her so he could enter.

"Linc, what is wrong with you?"

"Where is he, Sonja? I know he's still in here. I didn't see him leave."

Linc started for her bedroom. Instead of following him, Sonja sat down on the couch and waited for him to finish making a fool of himself. Five minutes later, he returned to the living room looking very foolish.

"I…I didn't see him leave, and my mind went crazy with all kind of images, of the two of you."

Sonja looked at him through tear-filled eyes. Why was he doing this to her? He didn't want her, or any other woman in his life. Sonja wiped at her tears as she stood and made her way over to the front door and snatched it open.

"Get out!"

"I…"

"Get out!"

Slowly Linc walked towards the door. He stopped in front of Sonja. As he looked at her, Linc didn't like what he found. She was shaking all over, and her beautiful face was covered with her tears. Once again, he had messed up. Slowly, Linc made his exit. Just as he stepped over the threshold, Sonja closed her front door tight. Linc turned and looked at the closed door. He placed his hand on the door as he spoke.

"Why do I keep doing this?"

Linc got in his vehicle and headed home. As he drove, Linc was going crazy with worry. For the first time in his life, Linc had found a woman that made him want to slow down. But all he seemed to do was hurt her. Linc was forty years old, and didn't know how to be in a relationship. Had he just put the last nail in his own coffin, or did he have a prayer left to fix this?

For a week straight, Linc had flowers delivered to Sonja at home and at work. He called her at least once a night. For the first few nights, she would pick the phone up and set it back down, hanging up before he could speak. Linc couldn't get too upset; he willingly took a few hang-ups, after what he had put her through.

♥

Lincoln was doing great in school. It was the middle of April, and the teachers were getting ready for performance reports, so Lincoln had a few days off from school. Lincoln asked his father if he could go see his mother.

"Hunter and I have a man watching her, trying to figure out her daily routine, but it seems her husband is always around. I should be hearing back from him. You know, why don't I call Uncle Hunter, and see if he's heard anything?"

"Could we Dad?"

"Sure."

Linc placed a call to Hunter. Hunter in turn placed his call. The man hired to be Connie's contact just happened to be with her when he took Hunter's call. With Linc on the other line, Hunter and the P.I. discussed spots they could possibly meet.

Before the trio ended their call, they had picked a place to get together. Young Lincoln wanted to see his mother, and his father was going to make that happen.

Two days later, Linc, Hunter, Kamrin and Tuesdae traveled with young Lincoln to secretly meet with his mom. Connie met them in an out of the way café. She told her husband she was going shopping for their daughter while little Kimberly was in dance class. So Connie didn't have much time to spend with her son. They visited for a while, and then it was time for Connie to leave. Before she left, Linc brought out the custody paper. Connie told Linc that she would be more than willing to sign custody papers as long as she could still have contact with their son. Linc agreed. As quickly as she arrived, she disappeared.

Young Lincoln was satisfied. His mother didn't have any new bruises; she looked fine. For the first time in his very young life, Lincoln Stone Jr. was a happy, normal young man. Linc was still a little worried about his son's mother. Linc wanted to know if Connie and her daughter were truly safe. Linc asked Hunter to pay Mr. Kim Vance a visit, try to get a feel on what this dude was capable of.

♥

Linc was becoming edgy. It had been so long since he touched Sonja. His body was beginning to ache for her. He desperately needed to kiss her lips. He couldn't take it any longer. Lincoln still had a few more days off from school, so his dad told him to pack a bag; they were going for a ride. He had someone special he wanted Lincoln to meet.

♥

Kamrin's divorce had been final for sometime now, but Tuesdae thought they should be taking things slower. Tuesdae wanted Kamrin to be sure he was ready for her.

On one of their weekends together, Kamrin and Tuesdae were hanging out downtown Indianapolis, when Kamrin took Tuesdae into a jewelry store.

"Why are we stopping here, Kam?"

"I need a few ideas. When it's time for me to pick out a ring for you, I want to get one I'm sure you will love."

Tuesdae pulled Kamrin to the side. She needed to speak with him privately. Something had been weighing heavy on her mind, and she needed to talk to him about it.

"Kamrin, I can point out as many rings as you like. But, I've been thinking. You've told me all about your ex-wife and what kind of life the two of you had."

"Yes, where is all of this going?" Kamrin was getting a little nervous.

She spotted the look of concern on his handsome face. Tuesdae needed to clear up that misunderstanding, and fast.

"No, no, no...I'm not trying to push you away Kamrin. I'm just suggesting we take a little time off. Not really off, just not spend as much time together. Look, Kam, you've just gotten out of a marriage that was ugly. Just because we feel this way about you each other now, doesn't mean it will last."

"So you're saying you might change the way you feel about us later?"

"No, but maybe you will. I think I will feel better knowing I haven't rushed you into this."

"Baby, what I feel for you is real, but if it's time you want, then it's time you will get."

Kamrin kissed Tuesdae's worries away.

"Now, you need to look at rings."

Chapter 8

Sonja had gotten through a few more weeks without Linc. She was missing him more with each passing day. She was in the kitchen preparing dinner for her boys and Dexter. It was Wednesday, and she hadn't cried since last Sunday. After the incident with Ty, Sonja didn't think she would ever want to look in Linc's face ever again. And then he started with the phone calls and the flowers. Sonja began to cave in. She started picking the phone up just so she could hear his sultry voice.

Ty had finished his job in town and was back in Arizona. Ty was nobody's fool. He knew something was going on between Sonja and the big man that was outside her front door that night. But he wasn't going to count himself out. Ty told Sonja that the next time he came to town, if she was still single, he was going to run her to the nearest courthouse and marry her. Sonja laughed. In jest, she told him that if she was still single, she would be waiting for him on the courthouse steps.

Matthew and Jeffrey had brought their X-box into the living room, and the boys were challenging Dex to every game they owned. It was almost five-thirty in the evening, and Sonja was in the kitchen preparing the salad. Dex was in the living room with the boys having a great time when the doorbell rang. At first Dexter waited for Sonja to come answer the door, but when she didn't, he answered the door for her. When he opened the door, there stood this well-built man who looked like he was straight out of a *GQ* magazine. Next to him was a younger version.

"Hello, can I help you?" Dexter stood in the door looking eye to eye with Linc.

"Who are you?" Linc was looking a little salty. How many men was Sonja going to entertain?

Sonja came out of the kitchen to see Dexter standing in the doorway talking to someone.

"Who is it, Dex?" Sonja came to stand next to Dexter. As Dex slipped his arm around her shoulder, Sonja could see Linc's jaw clinch. She was face-to-face with Linc, and a young man who looked just like him. She had so many questions, but they would have to wait. She asked the only one she could.

"Linc, what are you doing here?"

Linc kept eye contact with Dexter, but Dexter didn't back down.

"I wanted you to meet my son, Lincoln."

Words could not express the surprise that showed on Sonja's face. She took a good look at the young boy standing next to the man she was indeed crazy about.

"Well hello there. My name is Sonja. This is my neighbor, and his name is Dexter. Dex, will you go introduce this young man to my boys?"

Dexter still had his arm around Sonja's shoulder. "Are you sure you are all right?"

"I'm not going to hurt her!" Linc's words came out as if he couldn't stand the taste of them.

Sonja's whole body jumped at his affirmation. Because every time he touched her and then pushed her away, he hurt her.

Sonja looked at Dexter. "You don't have to worry, Dex."

Dexter kissed Sonja on the temple before leading the young man into the room to introduce him to Sonja's boys. After the introduction, the boys got along good. Matthew and Jeffrey were showing Lincoln all of their games. Before long, the boys and Dexter were playing and having a good time.

Sonja was trying very hard to be as nonchalant as possible as she headed for the kitchen. Linc was on her heels. Sonja hoped he couldn't see her body trembling. She wanted to hug him and slap him at the same time.

"So, would you and your son like to stay for dinner? I've made lasagna with garlic toast and a salad."

"Sure, if it's no problem? Baby, I need to talk to you."

"Linc, as much as I would love to hear the story behind the forthcoming of your son, I just don't think that we should do that right now."

In the kitchen, Linc went to stand behind Sonja. She was standing by the counter placing more garlic bread on the baking sheet. Linc placed his hands on either side of the counter trapping Sonja in.

"Love…"

The sound of his voice caused her to tremble. "I remember asking you not to call me that."

"Right, you did. You said people who used that word should only use it when there is meaning behind it. Well, love, I've found the meaning, I care deeply for you, Sonja."

Linc brushed his mouth across her ear and pressed in closer to her body.

"Baby, you are mine."

"Linc, please don't do this to me."

"Love, I have to. I've had things going on in my life that I've wanted to share with you. For the past few nights, it has been so hard not calling you, talking to you. I miss the sound of your voice. I miss the way you feel in my arms. Holding you while you sleep, baby, I'm sorry."

Linc pushed in closer and used an unsteady hand to push Sonja's hair away from her ear. His mind was whirling, and his body was experiencing things he'd never felt before meeting her.

Sonja found pleasure in the caress of Linc's hands in her hair, and he knew it. The contact from his strong fingers caused Sonja's eyes to close. She couldn't turn and look at him. Sonja was afraid if she faced him, this would turn out to be just a dream.

"Linc, the night we met I wasn't looking for a relationship. Over the years, I've come to believe that I'm not cut out for one. Besides, even if I were, you said it yourself you're not a one woman man. How did you put it? You're a playa for life. I don't want a playa in my life. I'm sorry, but I can't believe finding out you have a son has changed all of that for you. No, Linc, I'm not going to put myself through that. If

I'm going to be in a relationship again, I want a man who's ready and willing to devote himself to the relationship."

"Sonja, I've said a lot of things that I'm sorry for. And yes, you are right. I never wanted one special woman in my life, never wanted to put that much effort in a relationship. But after meeting you, I've found myself rethinking a lot of things. I want you in my life. I want to be your man. You don't have to look any further. I'm right here baby. Please give me a chance."

"What about all the other women?"

"I've turned in my playas card. I'm a one woman man. I haven't been with another woman since I had my first taste of you. Once I did, there was no going back. Baby, give me a chance. I want to make you happy. Come on, baby."

Sonja fought back her tears. "Since my husband passed away, I decided to devote my life to my children. Life was easier for me that way. Linc, I don't want to place my faith in you just to have my heart broken. I also have to think about my boys. They've been through enough. I won't have a man coming in and out of their lives."

"I won't let you or your boys down. Come on, baby. I need you. Will you at least say you will think about it?"

Sonja didn't say anything for a moment. Then she finally turned to face him. She needed to look in his eyes, only then could she tell if he meant all the words he was so easily tossing out.

"That first time we were together, you said that would be the only time. You kissed me, and all of my rational thoughts were blown away. My mind said no, don't do this, but I wanted to know. You've never been a one woman man, and I know I'm probably putting myself in a bad position."

Sonja took another moment to study him. Somehow she knew she was setting herself up to fall.

"If you hurt me again, or hurt my boys in any way, I promise to never speak to you, ever."

Linc pulled her into his strong chest and kissed her.

"Sonja, oh God, I've missed you. I'm sorry for everything, and you don't ever have to worry about any other woman. I don't want anyone but you. Oh baby. I thought I had lost you. Bear with me. This is all new to me, but I will do right; I promise."

Sonja couldn't help herself. She wanted him in her life. It didn't matter if it was right or wrong. Sonja's heart was beating so fast. Just to be close to Linc Stone drove her mad. It was still so hard for her to believe he wanted her. Linc was used to dating younger women who were single and childless, and much more sophisticated.

"We will see. Go finish setting the table. I need to put this bread in the oven."

Linc kissed her once more before he picked up the extra plates and place-settings. Smiling, he backed out of the kitchen. Sonja looked up to the heavens, and said, "Lord, please help us to make this work."

Ten minutes later, everyone was sitting down at the table. The conversation was based around video games. Sonja looked around her dining room table and smiled. Her good friend, Dexter, was there, her boys, and their new friend, Lincoln. Sitting next to her was Linc; the man Sonja prayed was the answer to her broken heart.

Just as everyone was finishing, Dexter got a phone call and needed to leave; something about work. He said his goodnights and headed out. After dinner, Linc and the boys volunteered to clean the kitchen.

Sonja stood in the doorway watching her men. Matthew and Jeffrey were acting as if Linc and his son had always been apart of their lives. Linc was up to his elbows in suds while the boys took way too much time drying them off and putting them away.

It was as if Linc could feel her presence, he turned to find her watching them. He smiled at her, and it momentarily made her weak.

"Sonja, you don't have a dishwasher?"

Sonja laughed. "I did, but she got married and moved out. Now I rely on these."

Sonja held up her hands. Linc wiped his hands on a towel and walked over to stand in front of her. He took Sonja's hands in his. He kissed them ever so gently. The boys found that to be quite amusing. Linc and Sonja could tell by all the laughter.

Once the dishes were done, Matthew and Jeffrey asked Lincoln to help them take their game back to the bedroom to hook it back up. Then they proceeded to beg their mother to let them play just one more game.

"Please, Mom, Lincoln hasn't played the matrix game yet."

Both boys encircled their mom's waist and looked up at her with their big beautiful eyes. It was very close to bed time, but Sonja gave in.

"You have thirty minutes."

Cries of joy floated through the house as Matthew and Jeffrey led Lincoln back to their room. Sonja and Linc went to the couch and sat down. Now she was ready to hear about Linc's son.

Sonja looked at Linc. "Do you want me to make some coffee?"

"No, love, I'm good." Linc pulled her in closer before he started talking.

"Remember when we first met, I told you about Connie, and how she had found someone else?"

"Yes."

"What I didn't tell you was a few years later we ran into one another. I think she and her boyfriend, at the time, were feuding, so she ran and jumped into bed with me. I only did it to confirm what I knew to be true. That I didn't need her like that anymore."

"Let me get this straight. You knew you didn't need to have sex with her any longer, but you slept with her just for the hell of it?"

"It doesn't sound right when you say it."

"That's because it's not right, Linc. Anyway, finish."

"Are you going to be upset with me about all of this?"

"No, that was in your past."

"Okay." Linc kissed her, and then looked into her eyes. He couldn't believe he had found his soul mate. Funny, he had told himself at a young age that he didn't have one. Linc knew she was his soul mate, because after he met her, his whole life changed.

"After you left me that morning, I was hit. My world was crashing around me. I was having a few drinks when I heard a knock on the door. I didn't want to answer. I knew it wasn't you. Well, whoever was knocking, they weren't going away. When I got to the door, I found Connie standing there, looking scared and worn out. Then there was this little mini-me standing next to her. Connie looks at me and says, "Linc, this is your son." Apparently, her husband doesn't like my boy and told Connie to send him away, or he was going to put my son out in the streets."

"He sounds like a winner. Where is Connie now?"

"Lincoln has a sister. Connie's husband won't let her have the girl, so Connie went back to him. She said she just wanted to make sure Linc was going to be all right."

"So what are you going to do?"

"Hunter and I got busy with paperwork. Lincoln started private school in Indianapolis. I am in the process of getting full custody."

"I think that's wonderful. I just hope Connie gets out of that relationship."

"The daughter has nothing to fear, so I don't think she will leave."

Sonja enjoyed watching Linc's face light up when he talked about his son.

"It feels good doesn't it? I know the two of you haven't had that much time together, but, it is a good feeling, being someone's parent."

"Sonja, never in my life did I think I would want to be a father. But when Connie showed up at my place, and in walked this miniature version of me, I just knew I didn't want him to grow up like I did. I know my father did his best, but it just seemed to LB and me , at the time, we weren't getting many father-son moments. Now I realize he did his best. It couldn't have been easy for him having to be the equivalent of two parents and the provider, while trying to keep up with our mom. And then he was snatched away from me and LB."

"It's plain to see, you are going to be a great father to Lincoln. He loves you so much already."

Just as Linc was ready to draw Sonja into his arms, the boys came running out of the room, pulling Lincoln with them.

Matthew spoke first. "Mom, can Lincoln spend the night with us, please?"

It was Jeffrey's turn. "Please, Mom. He can sleep in our room, and his dad can have in your room. "

Linc started to laugh. "Yeah, Sonja, I can sleep in your room."

Sonja hit Linc in the arm. "How about we have Lincoln sleep in the room with you guys, and his father can have sissy's room?"

They heard what they wanted to hear; Lincoln could stay. The rest was lost on their screams of joy.

"I will call the school and tell them Lincoln is visiting, and he can go to classes with Matthew. What about clothes?"

Sonja realized she was taking over.

"I'm sorry, Linc. Is that going to be all right with you?"

Linc looked at his son. "Lincoln, go get our bags out of the car."

"Yes, sir. Come on you guys; help me!"

As they ran to the front door to get their shoes and coats, Sonja pinched Linc.

"Ouch! What's that for!"

"You were planning on staying?"

He kissed her. "I was praying we could stay. God, baby, I've missed you."

"You're sleeping in Tiff's room!"

Linc smiled. "You can't blame me for trying."

Sonja and Linc let the boys watch one movie before going to sleep. They made sleeping mats on the floor. Since Lincoln was going to sleep on the floor, Matthew and Jeffrey wanted to also. Linc and Sonja changed the sheets on Tiffany's old bed and went back in the living room to talk for a little while longer. Linc decided it was time to give Sonja the full story about his parents.

Two hours later, Linc kissed Sonja goodnight. He wiped away her tears before she headed for bed. Her heart hurt for Linc and his brother, the nightmares they must have endured over the years.

Linc sat on Tiffany's old bed and wondered how he was going to get through the night with Sonja so close, but so far away.

Hours later, Linc went in to check on the boys. All three were fast asleep. He watched Lincoln sleep. God truly works in mysterious ways, he thought. Linc always said he never wanted children. Having only been with his son for a short time, Linc didn't want to be without him. Linc had sworn to never give his heart to another woman, but look at him now, sneaking around Sonja's house just to hold her in his arms, if only for a little while.

Man, Linc could finally see what his father and his brother were talking about. There's nothing like a good woman. Their father never really got to enjoy the love he had found, but it looks like Kamrin was getting another chance. And so was Linc. Life was good.

Linc ran his hand over his son's head before leaving the room. Then on silent feet, he found Sonja's bedroom. As he entered the room, he found her. She was lying in bed, and her eyes were closed. Linc went over to the bed and crawled in beside her. Sonja moaned and pushed in closer.

"Honey, I promise not to fall asleep in bed. I'm just going to hold you in my arms for a while, and then I will leave."

"Linc, I've missed you," was all she said.

Chapter 9

The next morning, Sonja woke to the smell of good things cooking in the kitchen. Grabbing her robe, Sonja made her way to the bathroom to brush her teeth and wash her face before entering the kitchen. As she stepped in, she found three little men sitting at the table, grinning and eating sausage and eggs while Linc washed dishes.

"Morning, Momma!" Matthew and Jeffrey both jumped up and went to give their mother a hug.

Sonja noticed Lincoln watching; she detected a little sadness in his eyes. Sonja cleared her throat and held out her arms to the boy.

"I guess my boys didn't tell you."

Lincoln's eyes grew two sizes. "Tell me what?"

"That I must have hugs in the morning."

Lincoln began to laugh. Sonja noticed Linc had stopped what he was doing and was watching them. He looked at his son and smiled. He decided to help him with his uneasiness.

"Let me go first!" Linc swiftly moved in and circled his arms around Sonja, Matthew and Jeffrey.

"Lincoln, you better come get some of this!"

Sonja could scarcely get the words out. Matthew and Jeffrey were laughing, because Linc was squeezing them tight. Through giggles, the boys called out to Lincoln.

Finally, he could stand it no more, Lincoln joined the family hug. Linc kissed Sonja on the top of her head and whispered a thank you to her for making his son feel welcome.

Matthew, Jeffrey and Lincoln sat back down at the table to finish their breakfast. Matthew looked at his mother and decided that since he was the oldest, he should speak for him and his brother.

"Mom, Jeffrey, Lincoln and I talked it over with Lincoln's dad. It's okay with us if Lincoln's dad is your new boyfriend."

Sonja looked over at Linc who was leaning against the counter, smiling.

"Yeah, I hope you don't mind. The boys and I talked about it this morning. They like the idea."

Sonja looked at her boys; they were all smiles. " If the vote has already been taken and everyone is in agreement, then I guess its official."

"Good! Love, I'm going to take the boys to school for you this morning. So sit down and enjoy your breakfast and your coffee."

"Are you sure, Linc?"

"Yes, baby, I'm sure."

Matthew and Jeffrey jumped up from the table and gave their mom kisses goodbye.

Sonja smiled as she watched her boys rush away calling for Lincoln to hurry along. Lincoln got up and quickly gave Sonja a hug and a smile before following Matthew and Jeffrey to the front door. Linc placed Sonja's plate in front of her and kneeled by her side.

"Do you think we have time for some lovin' before you have to leave for work?"

"I will make time."

Linc's face was handsome as he looked at her, his eyes were very serious. They were piercing and full of emotion. Sonja watched Linc as he ran his hands over her legs. He looked in her eyes with a passion that words could not convey, and it caused her to quake. Without a word, Linc got up and walked out of the room.

Half an hour later, Linc was entering Sonja's house ready to find his way home. Sonja had showered and put on Linc's jacket, the one he'd left in her room that February morning he came to her. She was waiting for him in the bedroom. Linc slowly entered the room and found Sonja sitting on the edge of the bed. He began to undress for her. Wearing nothing but his passion, Linc made his way to stand in front of her. The jacket she was wearing rested gently over her breasts. Linc pulled her up into his arms and kissed her with such hunger.

"Sonja, you're driving me crazy. I want us to take it slow baby. I need to love you slow and strong, but I'm so hungry for you. I've been starving for you for such a long time."

Linc moistened his lips before he recaptured her mouth again. He was determined to show her just how hungry he was. With strong hands, Linc pushed his jacket off Sonja's shoulders and stepped back to take in her delightfully feminine body.

"Sonja, you're so beautiful, and your skin is so soft. I could just devour you, baby. I will never grow tired of resting in your lusciousness. I'm so glad you belong to me."

Sonja turned her face from him.

"Love, what's wrong?" Linc stepped back to study her face.

"Linc, it's almost impossible for me to believe that I have this kind of effect on you. I represent everything you swore you would never have."

Linc moved in closer. He ran his hand through her hair and down her body, resting them on her backside. Linc lifted her sweet face to his own so she could look into his eyes. His voice was full of sentiment.

"Do you think I'm playin' with you?"

Sonja shuddered from his touch. "I...I don't want to think that. I want to believe that you really mean what you say, but you have to admit, I'm not like all the other women you've been with."

"You damn straight. You are a real woman, and you make my body come to life like only a real woman can. I really don't want to think about my past. Over the years I've been with a lot of chicken heads. For the first time in a long time, baby, with you, I find completion. You satisfy my appetite, when no other woman could. I'm so happy with you that I don't want to try and find out if another woman can. I have what I want in you."

Linc placed Sonja on the bed and covered her body with his own. Leisurely, he kissed her tears away and tenderly caressed her body. For what felt like an eternity, Linc handled her body boldly with his powerful hands. He whispered in her ear as he prepared to enter her.

"I'm yours, baby. Please forgive me for all the foolish things I did and said to you. I'm going home now, love. Are you ready?"

"Hurry, Linc." Sonja's body was screaming out to be pleased for the pleasure she had only experienced with this man.

Later, after the loving was done, Sonja was fast asleep next to Linc. She knew work was waiting for her, but Linc had put something on her. Her intent was to only close her eyes for a few moments. But he had put it on her so strong, and so good, even her eyelids were sedated. The phone rang, and Sonja couldn't move. Linc was fast asleep when it started ringing in his ear. Without thinking about it, he reached over and picked it up.

"Hello."

Nancy thought for a second that she had called the wrong number. She couldn't have; Sonja and Linc's numbers were nothing alike.

"Linc?"

"Hey, Nancy, what's up, babe?"

"I'm just looking for Sonja. Is she home?"

"Yeah, she's right here next to me."

"Okay. You want to tell me what's going on?"

"She and I are seeing each other."

"Wow. Okay, that's cool. Can I talk to her, or is she sleeping?"

"She's sleeping, but I can wake her, if you like."

"Well, I just wondered if she was going into the office today."

"Hold on, Nancy, you can ask her."

Baby, it's Nancy. She wants to talk to you."

Linc kissed her before handing her the phone. He then headed for the bathroom wearing absolutely nothing.

A very sleepy Sonja got on the phone. "Hi!"

"Girl, I know you can't talk right now, but as soon," as you can, you'd better call me and tell me everything!" She emphasized soon.

Sonja laughed at her friend. She knew Nancy wasn't kidding around.

"Ten, four!"

"Well, you might as well stay your tail home. You ain't gonna do me no good today. But you have to tell me this…the brotha can bring it, right?"

"Oh yeah, like no other. Brought tears to my eyes. It made me want to call my momma!"

"Damn! Well you handle your stuff!"

Linc re-entered the bedroom and climbed back in bed beside Sonja. Gently, he kissed her and removed the phone from her hand.

"Nancy, Sonja has something to do. Bye!" With that said, Linc hung the phone back up, and re-visited his favorite spot.

♥

It was two in the afternoon, and Linc was dragging his body out the door. He didn't want to leave her, but he needed to go to Sears. Sonja had washed her last dish. After he was done there, he would pick the kids up from school.

♥

Sonja soaked in a tub of hot water. Linc had loved her for hours, and now her body was rebelling on her. She didn't realize just how many muscles she used when making love to her man. The only thing she had been thinking about was how good he felt. And Linc felt wonderful. He undeniably knew what he was doing.

Sonja wondered how many women Linc had loved the way he made love to her. None, at least that's what he told her, and she was inclined to believe him. If he did to them what he did to her, they wouldn't waste time calling him. They would be camped outside his door every waking minute. Sonja knew she would have to start eating her Cheerio's and continue taking her vitamins so she could keep up with him. One thing was clear in her mind; Sonja was going to cater to her man.

Making her way through the kitchen, Sonja was preparing something for Linc and the boys to eat. As she looked at the clock, Sonja wondered what was keeping them. They were running over an hour late.

There was a knock at the front door. Sonja thought it might be Linc, but didn't he take a key? When she opened up the door, Dexter was standing there.

"Dex, what's going on? Do you want to stay and eat with us? Linc went to pick the boys up from school. They should be here soon."

Dexter walked in and headed for the living room. "Sonja, I want to talk to you for a moment."

"Sure, sit down and tell me what's on your mind."

"Look, you and your kids are like family to me. Arlando and I were good friends, and I think he would want me to look after you and the kids."

"What is this about?"

"I just finished talking to Ty. He asked about you, told me about the dude that he almost had an altercation with over you. When he described him to me, I knew right off it was the guy from last night. You guys have gone through enough. I won't sit back and let this dude hurt you or those kids."

Sonja placed her arms around Dexter's neck and was planting kisses on his cheek when Linc and the boys walked in. Matthew and Jeffrey were happy to see their friend. They charged at Dexter.

"Dex!"

Sonja moved just in time. As she moved to a safe place on the couch, she noticed Linc standing in the hallway, looking a little put out.

"Honey, what took you so long? I was getting worried."

Sonja walked over to Linc and his son. She gave young Lincoln a kiss on the forehead. Linc gave his son the bag so he could hold Sonja. Lincoln asked Matthew and Jeffrey to show him where to put the groceries. Sonja told them to finish and wash up, the food was done. Then she wrapped her arms around Linc's waist as she reached up to taste his sweet lips.

"Mmm, I missed you, honey."

Linc kissed her back, and then looked at her for a long time before turning his attention to Dexter.

"Hey, man, what's up? It's Dex, right?"

Dexter walked over and held out his hand to Linc. "Yeah."

Linc took his out stretched hand. "I brought some beer; you want have a Bud with me?"

"Sure, that sounds real good."

Sonja was happy to see them getting along. Just as everyone was headed for the kitchen, the doorbell rang. Sonja walked to the door to answer it. When she opened the door, she was speechless. There was a Sears truck in her driveway and two men standing at her door with a big box.

"Ms. Davis?"

"Yes?"

"We are here to install your new dishwasher."

Sonja turned to look at Linc. "What did you do?"

"I bought my baby a dishwasher." Linc pulled her in closer and whispered in her ear. "The only time I want those hands in water is when you're taking a bath with me."

"Linc!"

Linc smiled at the surprised expression on her face. "Move out of the way, woman. These men have other deliveries to make."

Sonja moved, and the men followed Linc into the kitchen to get right to work. The two guys were young, so Linc sent them in the living room with Sonja and the boys to play on the X-box while he and Dexter took over installing the appliance. Linc wanted to make sure it was hooked up right. An hour later, everyone had finished eating, and Linc and Dexter were showing Sonja and the boys how to work the new dishwasher.

Dexter and Linc sat and talked while they watched the boys play their new game, the one that Linc had been talked into buying. Sonja talked to Tiffany on the phone while everyone else was occupied.

"So, Mom, things are going good?"

"Very good, Tiff. I think the only other time I've been so happy was on the days I brought my babies into the world."

"Good. Terrell and I will be over tomorrow. I can't wait to meet Linc's son."

Sonja and Tiffany talked for a while longer. She told her all about the dishwasher. Tiffany talked to her brothers for a few minutes before she hung up. Dexter was telling the boys about a game he developed on his computer. They were so excited that they begged Sonja to let them go next door and look at it. Sonja said okay, and Linc walked the boys over to Dexter's house. He went inside and visited for a few minutes before going back to Sonja's. Dexter said he would bring them back in an hour.

When Linc came back inside, he went and sat next to Sonja on the couch.

"Linc, thank you for the dishwasher; you shouldn't have."

"I'm glad you let me do it. I thought for sure you were going to make them take it back."

"I might be crazy, but I'm no fool! Thank you, honey, really."

"I just want to make you happy. Besides, the boys said they were tired of washing dishes."

"It figures."

"Love, I want to talk to you about Dex."

"What about him?"

"I want you to know that when I walked in and found you kissing him, I almost lost it."

"Honey, I'm sorry. I didn't even think about that. Dex has been apart of this family for years. I would never do anything to hurt you. I bet the first thing that came to your mind was your mother? Oh, honey, please forgive me."

"It's cool, baby. I had to take a second to cool down. When you came to me and kissed me, I knew I didn't have anything to worry about. You didn't even think about it, you just reacted to my presence. At that moment, you made me feel like a king."

Sonja smiled up at him as she ran her hand across Linc's chiseled chin. "You are my king. You know you are my boo!"

Linc laughed at her slang and decided to use some of his own. "True dat. Dex and I talked, we're cool. He just wanted to know if I was for real."

Sonja smiled at him as she pushed her hand under his shirt and softly caressed his chest.

"Are you for real?"

"Girl, if you don't stop, you are going to find out just how real I am, when I pin you down on this couch and make sweet love to you."

Sonja wanted him, but her body was still aching. It needed a little more re-coupe time.

"Okay, I will behave. Tiffany and Terrell are coming over tomorrow. They want to meet Lincoln."

"Cool! Maybe we can take everyone to a movie and out to dinner."

"That sounds fun. When do you have to go back home?"

"I thought Linc and I would leave out Sunday night. I'm only going back because Linc has school. I don't know how I'm going to make it, being so far from you."

"I'm going to miss you too. But we have the weekends! Soon school will be out, and we can visit for longer periods."

"Visit my ass. You're coming to live with me for the summer."

"Linc, stop playing. You know I can't do that. What would the boys think of me?"

"I know, love. I'm just dreaming."

One hour later, Dexter walked the boys to the front door and said his goodnights. Sonja allowed Matthew, Jeffrey and Lincoln to pick out a short movie to watch before going to bed.

It was eleven o'clock before Sonja and Linc got the boys settled into bed. Linc headed for Tiffany's old room. He wanted to give the boys time to fall asleep. He got settled in bed and thought about his baby, how meeting Sonja had changed his life, significantly. Never in a million years did Linc ever think a woman, any woman, could change his mind on the way he felt about relationships. Committing himself to one woman was never in his plans.

It was so weird. From the first time he touched her at the New Year's party, Linc knew there was something special about her. Sonja was different than any other woman he had met. He had made himself stay away from her that night. That is until young Chad tried to make a move.

Sonja had thought it would matter to him that she had three children. Hell, Linc thought it was going to matter that she had kids. Her kids were lucky to have her, and she was made to be a mother. Now Linc was sure she was made for him.

It amazed Linc that he found it so easy to talk to her, be with her. He enjoyed just listening to her voice, it calmed him. With other woman, Linc never tried to talk to them. He never wanted to stay long enough to remember their names. But with Sonja, everything was new. Linc found he wanted things in his life he never dreamed of wanting. He was certain that if it were not for Sonja, and the part she played in his life, his son wouldn't be with him right now. Linc knew that if he hadn't opened his heart up to Sonja, he wouldn't be able to, or even want to, have a relationship with his son.

Rolling over, Linc noticed it was almost one in the morning. As he had done the night before, he entered the boys' room and checked on them. After he was convinced they were fast asleep, Linc headed for his love. Just as the last time, Sonja was asleep. Linc crawled into bed with Sonja and held her tight.

"What took you so long? I fell asleep waiting for you."

"Sorry, baby, I just wanted to make sure our boys were asleep."

"Mmm, I've missed your warmth. That stimulating scent your body gives off when you begin warming up. Touch me, honey, please."

Linc ran a possessive hand over her. "Sonja, what am I going to do without you, baby?"

"What are you going to do with me now?"

Sonja moved on top of Linc's strong body and tasted his sweet lips.

"Let me love you, Linc. Tell me what you want, what you like, and then just lay still and let me love you."

Linc told Sonja what to do, and she did as she was told. Linc lay as still as he could, under the circumstances. Sonja was working magic on his entire body, and, he loved it. With every touch, every kiss, every caress, Linc was falling fast and hard. He couldn't close his eyes; he had to look at her. The rapture that took form on her face just before they both came unglued was too much for him. Sonja collapsed atop his strong body. After kissing him, she thanked him for being in her life.

Linc's breath was coming quickly. Sonja had dropped it on him strong.

"No, thank you, love. I promise you, I'm not going anywhere."

Chapter 10

Soon after Linc and his son arrived home from Sonja's, Linc called the sporting goods store and had a gun cabinet delivered. Linc had a few guns that he normally left out for easy access. But, Linc wanted to be prepared because his son was with him now, and he knew Sonja and the boys would be spending a lot of weekends there. Lincoln and Sonja's boys weren't babies, but he didn't want to take any chances with their lives. Now they were locked away safe. He felt better about it, and he knew Sonja would, too.

♥

When Sonja made it into work that Monday, she had a surprise visit from Nancy. Nancy was thrilled that Sonja and Linc had become a couple. Nancy always knew Linc Stone was a good man, but he just needed to find the right woman. For the life of her, Nancy never envisioned that woman being Sonja. She could see Linc falling for Sonja, but Sonja falling for Linc? All that mattered now was that two of her good friends had found happiness together.

♥

That first week away from Sonja was long. Linc didn't think he was going to make it. But he did. When Friday finally came around, he had a car and a credit card waiting for Sonja. The car was in her driveway, and the credit card had been delivered to her at work with a note for her to call Linc as soon as it arrived.

"Linc, what is this?"

"It's a credit card in your name off of one of my accounts. When you get home, you will find a car in your driveway, waiting for you and the boys."

"Linc, I can drive my own car."

"You could, but I don't want you putting all those miles on your car. Not until I buy you another one."

"Linc, you're not going to buy me a car."

"We will see. The car has already been put on one of my other cards, so feel free to use that card whenever for whatever. Oh yeah, it has a ten thousand dollar limit, so do your thang, baby."

"This is too much, Linc."

"Sonja, love, I've only just begun to care for you. I miss you, baby, and I cant wait to feel your silky legs wrapped around me. Call before you take off."

"I will, and thank you, Linc."

♥

Tuesdae had lived in the same apartment complex for almost ten years now. Right after high school, she started working part-time for Save our Sons and Daughters, or S.S.D, while she attended college. It took some time, but Tuesdae obtained her degree in child psychology. Since that time, she has been putting it to good use in her community. The minds of young children intrigued her.

Tuesdae woke to the crisp smell of the Monday morning freshness in the air. After starting the coffee, she took a shower and put on a pair of sweats. Tuesdae poured herself a large mug of coffee and went down to get her mail. There were a handful of bills and a letter without a name or return address. She waited until she re-entered her apartment to open the letter.

As she sat at her small kitchen table, Tuesdae took another sip of her coffee. Once she had satisfied her taste buds, Tuesdae went for the unmarked letter, the bills could wait. After it was opened, she recognized the handwriting right away. It was from Milo Black. He said in the letter that he was going to be in town and wanted to see her. Ten years of emotions began to flood her mind. Milo. He had been her first, her only.

Before she met Kamrin, Tuesdae hadn't been in a serious relationship since the one with her old high school sweetheart, Milo Black. She knew she wanted to see Milo, but what would Tuesdae tell Kamrin about her visit with her old flame?

Milo Black had been the love of Tuesdae Parker's life for many, many years. From the young age of sixteen, Tuesdae and Milo had plans to marry. That was until Milo decided to join the military and make it his career. Tuesdae didn't want to move from place to place. She wanted to be stationary so she could have children. Milo had gotten it drummed into his head that he needed to serve his county.

Tuesdae tried for almost a year to sit back and wait for him. Out of nowhere, Milo wrote her a letter telling her he was releasing her from their promise. He told her in the letter that he had found someone in Korea; she was also a marine, and they were going to marry.

That was ten years ago, and she hadn't heard from him since. Kamrin was the first man that Tuesdae had been interested in since she received that letter so many years ago.

♥

Hunter got in touch with his friend Coy from one of the local news papers in Gary. Hunter explained his situation to the guy and asked him for help. The two made an appointment to interview the Vance family at work. Hunter wanted to see if Kim's family felt the same way he did about young Lincoln and his mother.

Hunter had been tailing Kim for a few weeks trying to see if he had a set schedule. This dude was sporadic; he didn't really have a schedule. The guy truly did nothing but show up to get his pay check. Hunter was certain that Kim and one of his employee's were having a fling, because he followed him to the same building more than once. Kim would stay inside for half an hour and then leave with a ridiculous grin on his face. Hunter was positive Kim's parents didn't know how their son was carrying on.

Hunter's reporter friend got an interview scheduled. Hunter and Coy would meet the Vance family in two days. Both the mother and the father were going to be there. They had been assured that Kim Vance would also be there and available for an interview. Hunter called Linc and informed him of his plans. Linc was on his way to pick Lincoln up from basketball practice.

"Linc, man, I got something for you."

"Cool, speak."

"I got us an appointment to interview the family at work. That's going to take place in two days."

"I'm on my way."

"No, you stay put. Let me handle this. Don't you have a woman to keep company with this weekend? After I get a feel for these people, I will get back with you. I don't want to set this dude off and make him take it out on Connie."

"You're right. I just got Sonja back, and I don't want to mess up again. I really want to get my hands on that fool, though."

"I know, man, but you have to think about Connie and her daughter."

"Okay, but as soon as you hit the door, call me, and tell me everything."

"I will. Hey, how is Kamrin holding up with his time away from his woman?"

Since Linc had Hunter focusing all his attention on Connie, he hadn't found much time to keep tabs on Kamrin. Hunter knew this time apart from Tuesdae was hard on the young brother.

"Good, he says he has faith in her love for him, and he's not giving her up without a fight."

"That sounds like a true 'Stone' statement."

♥

Hunter and Linc decided to keep Connie in the dark about their investigation of her husband. Hunter thought the less she knew, the better the chances were that she wouldn't get caught in the middle of something ugly. The last meeting Hunter and Connie had, he gave her full custody papers to sign and a progress report on her son. Hunter told Connie that the boy was doing great. Connie's eyes began to tear up with emotions. She missed her son terribly, but he was with his father, and he was safe.

Each time Hunter and Connie met, it was in some hole-in-the-wall bar. Connie needed to make sure Kim didn't find out what she was doing. Lincoln was in no way Kim's responsibility, but she just knew if he found out Connie took the boy to his father, where he would find love and affection, Kim would strike her again.

For reasons unknown to Connie, Kim just didn't like her son. Kim never met Lincoln's father, so he couldn't have anything against Linc. Kim had changed, especially over the last few years. Here lately he began acting strange, like he was hiding something. Connie couldn't help but think he was planning to take their daughter away from her.

♥

Kamrin was hanging out at his brother's, giving Tuesdae the time off she requested. He didn't need time, but if she needed space, he would give it to her. One thing was for sure, Kamrin and Tuesdae were going to be husband and wife.

A few days before she and Milo were to meet, Tuesdae finally told Kamrin about her past, about the letter she received from Milo, that he wanted to meet with her. Kamrin couldn't lie. He was threatened by Milo Black, and his sudden, grand entrance back into Tuesdae's life. Kamrin tried not to let the fact that Tuesdae never mentioned the close relationship the two shared, bother him. Instead, he kept reminding himself that he believed in their love, and he believed in Tuesdae.

Kamrin stretched out on his bed with his eyes closed. He was picturing in his mind Tuesdae's sweet face as they spoke on the phone.

"Kamrin, are you sure you're okay with me seeing Milo by myself?"

"Do you plan on doing something with him?"

"No! Why would you ask me something like that?"

"You just seem a little too nervous to *just* be going to see him. Look, Tuesdae, I trust you, you trust me. Isn't that how it goes?"

"Yes, Kam. It's just that he was once a very important person in my life. We were going to get married."

"Tell me something, baby. If it was that serious, then why wait until now to tell me about him?"

"I don't know. I guess so many years had pasted that I didn't think I'd ever see him again. So, why worry you with it?"

Kamrin decided not to play games, he had to know. "This thing with him was a long time ago, but maybe you should ask yourself if you still love him?"

Tuesdae took a moment to think about it. She had so many old memories running around in her mind every since she had gotten that letter. She closed her eyes for a second and tried to imagine what her life would be like if she and Milo had married. Then she thought about the life she had been dreaming of with Kamrin.

"You know, if someone had asked me that question before I met you, I would have said, 'Maybe, I'm not sure.' Knowing that you and I share this special love for one another, I can proudly and honestly say no, I don't love Milo anymore. I love you, Kam."

"I like hearing you say that. I wish I were there so I could hold you in my arms. We are still on our break, right?"

Tuesdae smiled. She knew what Kamrin was waiting to hear. "Yes, but I think we can put an end to that after this week. Let's plan on having a special night together next weekend."

"That sounds like a good idea. I mean, we should do something special since it's your birthday!"

"Kam! How did you find that out? Who told you?"

"Baby, it's my job to know everything about you. I must admit, this Milo thing did slip by me."

"Honey, you have nothing to worry about. Don't you remember? I said I plan on having you, Kamrin Stone. Mark my words; you will be mine."

Before ending their call, Kamrin and Tuesdae discussed the plans Kamrin had for her birthday. They agreed that Linc and Sonja should join them in Chicago to celebrate. Kamrin would also tell Hunter to find a date, because he wanted him there, too.

♥

Connie couldn't believe it. She was pregnant. What was she going to do? Should she keep it from Kim? No, it wouldn't take him long to find out. He kept a good record of her monthly cycles. Kim had been over bearing when they first married, but now he was obsessive and controlling. Even more so, now that Connie had sent her son away. Kim thought the boy was with his grandparents.

♥

Bright and early in the morning, Milo Black was waiting for Tuesdae in her office. She was surprised to see him. They had lunch plans, so she wondered why he was there so early.

"Tuesdae, baby girl, you look good. You haven't changed a bit! Come here and give me a hug."

She looked at Milo; he looked good, too. He was in his uniform, all decked out. His jacket was loaded with medals of Honor, , Marksmanship ribbon, and so many more. Milo Black was now a high ranking officer in the Marine Corp.

"Milo Black! Oh, Milo, it's been too many years. How are you?"

Tuesdae walked into his open arms and gave him a nice hug.

"I'm good, lil' bit! I can see you are doing what you always dreamed of. So, word on the street is you've talked yourself into a new building."

Her smile was bright as she answered. "Yes, I did. I think it's going to be great for the kids. You've been here long enough to talk to people on the street, huh? What took you so long to contact me?"

"The truth is this was just a layover. I'm getting ready to leave. My orders are in, and I'm being sent on a covert mission."

"So you are still in that special task force?"

"Yeah, I love it. Sometimes it gets pretty dangerous, but that's half the fun."

"How does your wife feel about all of this?"

Sadness crept up onto his face. "Yeah, about my wife, I've wanted to talk to you about that for so many years. But for so long I was embarrassed, I couldn't stand to think about it. I wasn't ready to share it with anyone. Especially you, lil' bit, not after the way I sprung our marriage on you."

"What is it, Milo; did something happen to her?"

Milo walked over to the window and stared out into space. He told himself he could do this; he could talk to Tuesdae about this. Tuesdae moved to stand next to him. She looked into his handsome face. Tuesdae had always thought she and Milo would spend the rest of their lives together. The truth is, it had only been puppy love between them. She was certain Milo had realized it when he met his wife and found real love.

"I had it all worked out in my head what I was going to say. I've known for a few years that I wanted to talk to you about it. It's been so hard for me to get through it."

"Milo, if it's going to hurt you to tell me, then don't. You don't owe me anything."

Milo turned to look at his friend: beautiful, trusting, and always willing to help. So many times after Lolita left him, Milo wanted to contact Tuesdae. He felt that she wouldn't want to hear from him. Not after the way he had ended their relationship.

"I don't want to go into great detail, but I do want you to know that Lolita and I never married."

"What? What happened?"

"Lolita and I had this on again off again thing. We kept it our little secret; if anyone had found out we would both be in deep trouble. After one night of drunken passion, we went our separate ways not wanting our affair to go public. Shortly after, Lolita found out she was expecting our child. We talked and decided she would retire early and we would get married. She spoke with her commanding officer and requested to come out of the field and to be given a desk job. "

"So you have a child?"

Milo's voice broke as he spoke. "No, she miscarried. After her miscarriage, she talked to me, said it was fate. Lolita said we were never meant to be together."

"So, you never married?"

"No."

Tuesdae watched as Milo let his tears fall. She knew they were tears for his unborn child, and his lost love. Gently she pulled him into her embrace.

"Milo, you don't have to talk about it anymore. It's too painful, and you've been through enough."

Milo pushed his tears away as he held on tight to his friend.

"Tuesdae, so many times I wanted to call, or write, tell you I was sorry and to beg you to please take me back. Instead I got involved with the Special Forces and took the first assignment that was far, far away."

"You ran?"

"You damn straight. I didn't even blink. It was too hard to face Lolita, after the death of our child, and to know that we were only going to marry because of the baby. At least that's what she says. It was hard to know how to feel. I mean, should I have felt hurt or relieved?"

"Oh, Milo, what a thing to live with. I'm sorry for your loss. I wish you would have come to me sooner."

"I'm going to be okay. I know that when I'm done healing, He will bless me again, if I allow Him to."

"No matter what has happened between us in the past, we were once good friends and because of that, I will continue to pray for you, Milo."

"Thank you, lil' bit. You know, when I got in town, it was my intention to try and get back with you. But after I talked with a few folks and got the 4-1-1, I decided it was better for me to be happy for you rather than to come here and start up trouble for you and your man. I hear he's a good one, treats you real fine."

"I know what I've found in Kamrin is what I've always been looking for. Once you decide to slow down, you will find that one special woman who was designed just for you. Milo, after I got that letter from you, telling me you were getting married, I almost shut down. But I couldn't, there were too many kids who needed me out there. I knew you wouldn't want me to shut down. You expected me to pick up and move on. So I did. We were so young, but what we had was good. Milo, we learned a lot together. I will always consider you a good friend."

"I'm on my way out of the country, and I'm not sure when I will be returning. I had to see you before I left. I wanted to make sure you had gone on with your life. I always thought I had hurt you deeply. I'm happy to see you didn't falter; you moved on. Hey, tell this new man in your life that he is one lucky guy. Lil' bit, I will forever be grateful for your friendship."

Tuesdae was happy Milo had come to see her. She wasn't worried about cheating on Kamrin; she knew she loved him. Seeing Milo again finally gave her closure from that chapter of her life, forever. Now she was ready to start anew with Kamrin.

♥

Sonja and the boys pulled into Linc's driveway. Young Lincoln came barreling out the front door grinning so hard it looked as if it might hurt.

"Matt, Jay!"

Matthew and Jeffrey couldn't get their seatbelts off fast enough. They jumped out of the truck, and the three boys burst into laughter as they collided into one another. Linc stood on the porch and watched them. Linc looked so happy. Once the boys were done saying hello, Linc came off the porch and went to open Sonja's car door.

"I guess they are happy to see each other."

Sonja laughed as she watched the boys bounce inside. "Yeah, I would say so."

Linc took Sonja and the boys on a tour of the house. They breezed through Kamrin's room and Linc's office, and ended up in Lincoln's room. Linc allowed Tuesdae to remodel the room for the Lincoln.

The first thing Sonja noticed was the picture of Linc, Connie and Lincoln sitting next to the boy's bed. Connie was indeed a beautiful woman, more beautiful than Sonja imagined her. Sonja's stomach tightened when she looked at the way Linc was holding onto Connie as he gazed upon her beautiful face. They looked so good together.

Sonja's mind began to wander. Ugly things from her past tried to surface. What did Linc really see in her? After being with someone like Connie, how did Sonja measure up? Sonja couldn't help but think that once the thrill of their lovemaking was old to Linc, would he head back to Connie now that she has found a place in his life again?

After the tour, Linc showed the boys the backyard. Linc grilled burgers and hot dogs on the deck while the boys hung out in the Jacuzzi. Once they were fed, Lincoln took Matthew and Jeffrey inside to dry off and show them the inflatable mattress beds his dad had bought for the three of them. The boys camped out in the living room, Linc slept in Lincoln's room, while Sonja slept in Linc's bed.

When Linc took her in his room to help her put away her things, Sonja was shocked to find the clothes she had brought with her the first visit. They were inside his dresser drawer.

That first night Linc didn't try to visit her, but he had big plans for them the next.

The next day Linc had a full day planned out for those boys. It was his intention to wear them out. Linc and Sonja followed behind the boys as they made their way through the museum. Then they sat behind them at the movie theater. After they went to the museum and the movie, they went out to eat. Once they were home, Linc took the boys and they played ball in the backyard.

The boys were slowly wearing down. Linc let them sit in the Jacuzzi for a while. When they were tired of that, they went to Lincoln's room and played a few games. Close to midnight, three little engine's began to shut down. It wasn't long before they were knocked out.

Well after midnight, Linc ran a nice hot bubble bath for him and Sonja. There were scented candles all around the bathroom, and the late great Luther Vandross was serenading them.

Linc locked the bedroom door, then undressed before removing Sonja's clothing. Once done, he proceeded to make love to her on the chaise lounge next to his large oak armoire as the moonlight spilled in through the window, bathing their joined bodies. Then he moved them to the bathroom floor. Giving her time to catch her breath, it was time to try out the bathtub.

After making love to her in the tub, Linc then picked Sonja up and dried her off before placing her in bed. There Linc studied her as he ran his hands freely over her body. Pleasing her was all he wanted to do.

Linc had only been in one relationship before Sonja, and that had been with Connie many years ago. Life after that was just a blur, too many women to try and remember. Linc wanted to make sure he was treating Sonja right, the way she deserved. He took another moment to study her as she lay next to him. A warm sensation flowed through him, because he knew she was all his. He felt a little foolish asking, but he just had to know.

"How am I doing, Sonja?"

"What? My eyes rolling to the back of my head isn't answer enough?"

Linc couldn't contain his laughter. "Woman, I'm not talking about our love making! I'm talking about me, being your man. Am I doing a good job?"

Sonja placed her hand on his handsome face, while looking into his light eyes.

"Linc, I want you to know that I appreciate everything you do for me and my boys. I don't want you to think you have to spend a lot of money on me to make me happy. Just being with you gives me so much joy. Yes, I think you are doing a terrific job. I'm lucky to have you."

"I just want to do right by you, baby. I haven't had one special woman in my life since Connie. Love, I just want to make you happy."

Sonja winced at Linc's comparison to both relationships. "You do, Linc. How am I doing?"

Linc kissed her like it was as common to him as breathing. Once the kiss ended, he got a smirk on his face as he looked reflectively into her dark brown irises.

"You are more than I deserve. Oh yeah, about that eye rolling thing. It's impossible for me to see your eyes if mine are in the back of my head."

Sonja gave him a double take just before she burst into laughter.

"Hush, woman, are you trying to get those boys in here? I'm not done with you yet."

Their weekend had gone by fast. Sonja and the boys were getting ready to head out soon. Linc and Sonja were sitting on the couch watching the boys play cards. Linc's cell phone rang. As he looked at the display screen, he jumped up from the couch and called out for Lincoln to follow him. They headed for one of the back rooms. It was obvious he and his son needed to talk to this person in private.

After the call, Linc never told Sonja that the caller was Lincoln's mother, but she heard Lincoln telling Matthew and Jeffrey that he had just spoke with his mother. Sonja wasn't sure why Linc didn't want to talk to her about Lincoln's mother. All of his secrecy was beginning to hurt her feelings. She was the woman in his life now. She should share everything with him, right?

♥

Hunter and Coy, from the local newspaper, arrived at Vance Supplies. Today was Coy's day off. He was doing Hunter a big favor. Coy figured he would take some notes, because there could actually be a story here. The Vance family owned a handful of office supply stores. Mr. and Mrs. Vance, along with their son, ran the main office.

There were about twenty employees in the building responsible for taking orders and making sure they arrived at their destination on time. Kim's parents handled the financial part while Kim was in charge of the employees. Since he had an office manager, along with two supervisors, there wasn't much for Kim to do, except sit at his desk surfing the Net.

As the two men entered the classy two-story building, they were greeted by the receptionist. Coy informed the woman that the Vances were expecting them. She checked her appointment book on her computer and asked the men to follow her. As they made way to the elevator, Hunter noticed Kim Vance's name on one of the office doors. There was an attractive young woman sitting at the desk outside the door. The receptionist stopped at the elevator door and told them that when they got to the next floor, Mr. and Mrs. Vance's secretary would be waiting for them.

Hunter was surprised to see the young-looking couple exit from one of the offices. The Vances didn't look a day over fifty. The interview went on for about thirty minutes. Hunter had given Coy a list of questions he wanted him to ask the couple.

He found out that the couple was told they couldn't have children. About a year later, Kim came along. They felt he was a gift, so they gave their son whatever he wanted. Mr. Vance said they later realized it was a mistake. Their son was a good person, just a little lazy.

They spoke lovingly about their daughter-in-law and her son, and how happy they were when Connie and Kim gave them a granddaughter to go with their grandson. Mrs. Vance said she missed Lincoln, and she couldn't wait for the boy to get back from his visit with his other grandparents.

Bingo! That's what Hunter wanted to know. They had no idea Kim struck the boy and put him out of the house.

Mr. and Mrs. Vance decided to walk Hunter and Coy down to their son's office. Along the way, the Vances told little stories of Kim's childhood. As they got off the elevator, everyone noticed Kim's secretary wasn't at her desk. Mrs. Vance spoke.

"I'm not sure where the young lady that sits at this desk is. Let's go on inside Kim's office."

Mrs. Vance turned the knob and entered the office. As she turned to look at her son's desk, her steps faltered. Mr. Vance stepped in front of his wife and shielded her eyes. His voice was boisterous.

"Kim, what is going on here?"

Kim's secretary almost bumped her head on his desk as she moved to get up. Coy and Hunter looked at one another. Hunter smiled as he spoke.

"Well! We can see you are hard at work!"

Coy chimed in, moving his hands as if he were hitting a drum.

"Ba-dump-bump!"

The woman quickly fastened her blouse and wiped her mouth while Kim tried to hurriedly fasten his pants back up. Kim's mother and father were mortified. Mr.

Vance held his wife in his arms as he spoke.

"Young lady, pack your things. You are no longer employed here!"

The girl was shaken. She looked at Kim and waited for him to jump to her defense. He didn't.

"Kim, tell them, tell them! You said if I slept with you, I wouldn't lose my job. You wouldn't allow it. Tell them, Kim!"

Mr. Vance got on the phone and called for security. He wanted the young lady removed from the building.

Kim wouldn't look at his parents, but he did look at the two men with them. Dammit, one was from the local paper, but who was this other guy? Kim intended to find out.

Chapter 11

Linc and Lincoln were on their way to Dowagiac. Lincoln was so excited. He was going to spend the weekend with his two best friends. The ride there went fast, because Linc and his son spent the whole time talking. Lincoln told his father that even before his mother married Kim, he never really had any friends. He spent the majority of his time with his mom. Linc thought about Matthew and Jeffrey; the boys never once treated Lincoln indifferent. From the very start they welcomed Linc and his son with open arms.

When Linc and his son arrived at Sonja's house, Tiffany and Terrell were already there. Linc had asked Tiffany and her husband if they would keep his son and her brothers so he and Sonja could spend the weekend in the Windy City. Tiffany and Terrell were happy to help. Sonja told them to stay at her house so the boys would have plenty of room to romp about. Linc, despite Sonja's protest, rented a truck for Tiffany and Terrell to haul the boys around in.

Sonja gave out the house rules, and Linc wrote down his cell phone number. After getting the boys to stop playing long enough to give out hugs, Linc and Sonja were on their way to Chicago. All they had to do was arrive. Kamrin had made hotel reservations for Linc, Sonja and Hunter, and whoever was lucky enough to spend the weekend with Hunter.

♥

Hunter was sitting inside Pieper Hollow's small apartment. He was waiting for her to finish packing. It had taken him more time than he would have given any woman to agree to spend the weekend with him. Hunter had different rules than other playas. He actually enjoyed spending the night, even the weekend. He couldn't remember ever having to give a woman time to think about whether or not she wanted to go with him.

Hunter had met Pieper over a month ago one morning at his favorite coffee spot, where she served him his cappuccino. Hunter had frequented that same coffee house for years. Until a month ago, he had never seen her there before.

Pieper was different than any other woman Hunter had ever run into. When Hunter began to show his interest in her, she seemed to look right past him. Pieper always appeared to have something on her mind. Hunter even entertained the thought that maybe she were hiding something, or possibly running from something or someone.

Pieper was a tiny young woman whose hair was cut very short. Hunter didn't normally go for any woman he couldn't grab himself a hand full of hair in the heat of passion. After asking her out twice and being turned down, he was on a mission. For two weeks straight, Hunter made an appearance in the coffee shop. Finally, his persistence paid off. When she finally said yes, Hunter had decided he would compromise on the hair thing. He would work something out.

Hunter was deep in thought, thinking about some of those compromising positions he could put Pieper in when her soft voice broke his train of thought.

"Hunter, I'm not sure I should be going away with you for the weekend."

Hunter got up off the small couch that was in the petite one bedroom apartment, and walked over to where Pieper was standing. Her skin was dark and smooth, and she had a small beauty mark right in the middle, between her eyebrows. Hunter wanted to cuddle with her and taste those lips. She was holding onto her suitcase. Hunter gently took the bag from her soft, tiny hands.

"Pieper, come on, it's going to be fun. I promise you will have a good time, and I won't do anything you don't want me to."

"I've never been to Chicago before, and it does sound like fun."

"Good, come on. We need to hit the road. Kamrin and Linc are probably waiting for us."

♥

Three hours after leaving Dowagiac, Linc and Sonja pulled in front of the hotel where Kamrin had reserved rooms for everyone. Kamrin and Tuesdae were already there. They met Linc and Sonja in the lobby. Hunter and his date would be joining them soon.

"Happy Birthday, Tuesdae. Hey, LB, how are you doing?" Linc hugged his brother and then gave Tuesdae a quick squeeze.

Kamrin smiled at Sonja. "Hi, Sonja. I want you to meet my girlfriend, Tuesdae Parker. Baby, this is Sonja Davis; Linc's woman."

The two women smiled as they shook hands. Linc and Kamrin were happy to see the two women were going to get along just fine.

Kamrin and Tuesdae's plans included a trip to a movie house. The Viewing Room was one of those places that served dinner during the movie. After a movie and dinner, they were headed to a jazz club.

Tuesdae was involved with all of the plans, except one. When they arrived at the jazz club, Kamrin's plan was to ask her to marry him. The three-carat yellow diamond incased in a wide platinum band was safe in his pocket. This was the ring Tuesdae kept trying not to look at.

Kamrin and Tuesdae went to their room after Linc and Sonja checked in. Linc and Sonja wanted to get their things put away and take a few minutes to rest. Once Linc and Sonja reached their room, his cell phone rang; it was Hunter. They were close. Linc gave Hunter the address of the movie house. Once Hunter and his date arrived, they would check into the hotel and take a cab to The Viewing Room.

♥

Today Kim did what he had been doing for the past few days He was home early, and he wasn't in a good mood. Every since that incident with his secretary, his parents have been riding him pretty hard. Connie wasn't happy to see him. For the past three weeks, Kim had her walking on pins and needles. Connie still hadn't told him she was pregnant. And she wouldn't get the chance to tell him today, either. Kim took a quick shower, changed clothes, and played with his daughter for a few minutes just before he left.

♥

Sonja found she was experiencing so many new things with Linc. She was beginning to realize just how sheltered and boxed in she kept herself. This was her first time going to a place like The Viewing Room. Their hotel room was fantastic. Sonja had never been to one so ritzy.

Kamrin had already purchased everyone's tickets for the movie. They would pay for their meals later. They were still waiting on Hunter and his date. The place was starting to get crowded, so Kamrin and Linc went to find seats for them while they waited. Linc and Kamrin came back with three chairs. First Kamrin sat down, and as if on cue, Tuesdae took her place on his lap.

Linc then took his seat, but much to Linc's surprise, Sonja tried to sit in the empty chair.

"Love, what are you doing?"

Sonja was confused. She hoped Linc didn't expect her to sit on his lap, too. Tuesdae was a little thing. She was at least thirty pounds lighter than Sonja. Sure, Linc was probably twenty pounds heavier than Kamrin, but Sonja wasn't going to put Linc's leg to sleep.

"I'm saving Hunter's seat."

Linc pulled Sonja up from the chair. With slight force, Linc placed her on his knee. She was embarrassed, but Linc wasn't going to let her be. He ran his hand down her back until she started to loosen up. Then he used his other hand to bring her head towards his. He kissed her, and then whispered so that only she could hear him.

"Relax, baby; you're with your man."

The waitress came to take their drink order. Kamrin ordered wine for Tuesdae and a beer for himself. Linc got himself whiskey, and he ordered Sonja a strawberry daiquiri. Just before the waitress could leave, Hunter and his date arrived.

They greeted everyone as Hunter pulled out the chair that had been saved for him and sat down. He then held out his hand to Pieper. At first he didn't think she was going to take it. Pieper looked at the other women. She slowly took Hunter's hand and let him guide her onto his lap. The waitress took their orders. Hunter got a Rum and Coke, and Pieper asked for the same.

"Everyone, I want you to meet my date, Pieper Hollow. Pieper, this is Kamrin and his woman Tuesdae. We are here for her birthday. Tuesdae, are you having a good time?"

Tuesdae nodded a silent hello to the young woman before answering Hunter.

"Yes, thank you, Hunter."

"Good. Pieper, this is Linc and his woman Sonja."

Pieper spoke to everyone, and she began to relax. She knew it was going to be a fun weekend.

The food and the movie had been excellent. Now they were off to the jazz club. Everyone piled into Kamrin's SUV. The conversation was light and fluid the whole ride. On arrival, Kamrin found a parking spot after he let the women out at the door. As Sonja, Tuesdae and Pieper entered the club, they were impressed. The atmosphere inside was astonishing. Then the three men hurried inside to their dates.

Kamrin spoke briefly to the hostess before she led them to a table up front. As they were walking to their table, Sonja noticed a young woman pointing at them to another girl. Her stomach got a sharp pain. Somehow she just knew what was going to happen.

Across the room, Vera couldn't believe her eyes. It was Linc Stone in the flesh. What was he doing in Chicago? Who was that woman with him? She had to be an old friend, because Linc Stone couldn't be involved with that woman.

The night was going along smooth. Kamrin was getting close to his big moment. Linc was still oblivious to the young woman staring at them, but Sonja was waiting for something to happen. Hunter and Pieper had just walked onto the dance floor when Vera made her presence known.

"Linc, honey, what are you doing here? How have you been?"

The young woman practically sat in his lap, but she didn't get very far. Linc pushed her away before he stood up. Linc brushed at his clothing as if to remove any imprint she may have left on him. The only woman he wanted touching him was Sonja.

"Hey, hey, I'm here with my woman. Do yourself a favor and go back over to your friends. I don't really care where you go, but don't come back over here again."

With that, Linc took Sonja by the hand and headed for the dance floor, leaving Vera standing, watching their backs.

Linc pulled Sonja in close as they danced. "Sorry, love. Are you okay?"

"I knew it would happen sooner or later."

"Baby, I'm sorry. I don't want anyone to mess up our weekend."

Linc pulled her in closer to his hard body as he ran his large hands through her hair. Usually that helped her to relax. Normally, she melted at his touch, but not this time.

Linc could still feel the tension rushing through Sonja's body.

"Damn. Baby, do you want to leave?"

"And make that little tramp think she can run me away?"

"That's my girl." Linc kissed her slowly.

After the music stopped, Linc and Sonja found their way back to the table right behind Hunter and Pieper. Hunter decided to talk business.

"Since we are all here, I want to talk about the fundraiser party for the building. It's scheduled in two weeks. Then we have the dedication for the building the week after."

Tuesdae was excited. She was more than ready to move to the new building. Hunter had been busy with the "Kim Vance" thing, but he and Tuesdae brainstormed every chance they got to get this fundraiser off and running.

Linc looked at Sonja. "Are you going to be able to make it back in two weeks?"

"I don't think so."

Linc didn't look pleased. "What do you mean? Is it because of the girl earlier?"

"No, Linc. Tiffany and Terrell have plans."

"Oh." He looked away from her. He realized something; this would be their first weekend apart.

An older man stepped out on the stage and called out, "Is there a Tuesdae Parker in the house?"

Tuesdae looked over at Kamrin. She knew he had put the man up to getting her on stage, just so they could sing Happy Birthday to her. Smiling, she stood and made her way to the stage. Another man came onto the stage carrying a chair for Tuesdae to sit on. She took her seat. Tuesdae wasn't surprised to see a microphone in his hand. She was prepared to hear the birthday song. Instead, the man began singing Luther Vandross's song, "If Only for One Night." He sang a few notes before Kamrin stepped onto the stage and kneeled before her.

Shock registered on her face as Kamrin took her hand into his. The music stopped, and the man lowered to microphone toward Kamrin's mouth.

"Tuesdae, I could never be happy with just one night, baby. I want eternity. I want you to proudly take my last name. I want you to carry my children inside your appetizing body. Baby, will you please make my life complete? Will you marry me?"

Kamrin had truly caught her off guard. It took her a moment to find her voice. "Yes!"

For the next few hours, the three couples partied. They finally ended up back at the hotel in Kamrin and Tuesdae's room. The suites were large. When they entered the hotel room, they walked into a small living room that led to a modest kitchen area. The men stopped in the kitchen and pulled out some beer. They went to the table and began talking about Connie and Kim. Linc could still feel tension vibrating off Sonja.

Tuesdae and the two women stayed in the living room area. They sat drinking glasses of wine as they talked about Tuesdae's ring and how surprised she was.

Linc looked into the other room at his woman. She was his heart. Tonight his past had hurt her. He said a silent prayer, hoping that once they got to their room, they would talk about it.

"Linc, man, you would have enjoyed watching that fool try to zip his pants up while his parents were screaming at him."

"Screwing the help; this dude is messed up." Linc couldn't believe what he was hearing. With a woman like Connie waiting for him at home, why would he go out whoring?

Hunter was in full agreement. "Yeah, this Kim was a real piece of work. It seems to me he has conjured up in his tiny little mind, a love-hate thing for Connie. It doesn't seem to stop even though Lincoln is gone."

Kamrin was getting just as concerned for Connie's well being as Linc was. Sure, she did some things in her past, but Connie was a good woman. She deserved a good life. He wondered if Connie's husband had found the legal papers concerning the custody of Lincoln.

"He didn't get a look at the custody papers, did he?"

"Connie didn't say anything, but maybe she doesn't know he found them."

Linc became worried. "Hunter, man, as soon as you can, please find out. I don't want this dude using her as his punching bag again."

Sonja was getting a headache. She knew the three men were discussing Connie. First the woman in the club, and now Connie; she needed to go lay down. Sonja got up from her seat and told the other women that her head was hurting. Sonja walked over to the table where the men were sitting and told Linc she was going to their room.

"Do you want me to come with you?"

"No. Stay and finish your discussion. I will be fine."

Tuesdae spoke up. "We will walk her to the room, Linc. You don't have to worry. She is in good hands."

Sonja gave Linc a quick kiss and practically ran out the door. Ten minutes later, Tuesdae and Pieper walked back in the room to find the three men had moved to the living room and were watching some sports channel.

Tuesdae went and sat on Kamrin's lap, and Pieper sat next to Hunter. Linc had been leaning against the wall, thinking about Sonja. He decided he had given her enough time to calm down.

"Okay, you guys; I think I'm going to turn in with Sonja. See everyone in the morning."

As Kamrin was getting up to walk Linc to the door, Hunter and Pieper decided they would turn in also. Everyone was going to meet in the morning for breakfast. Kamrin and Tuesdae walked them to the door and said their goodnights.

Linc entered the room. Sonja had left a light on for him. Linc headed right for the bedroom. Inside, he found Sonja positioned on the bed. She was buried under the covers with her back to him.

He stood next to the bed, hoping she would turn around and look at him. She didn't.

He spoke, in hopes that Sonja would shift and face him so they could talk.

"Hey."

Sonja kept her back to Linc as she spoke.

"Finished with your business, huh?"

There was no tenderness in her voice. Linc answered and turned towards the bathroom to take a shower.

"Yeah."

♥

Hunter and Pieper entered their room, and she headed straight for the shower. Hunter looked around the room Kamrin had reserved for the couple. Kamrin had assumed that a room with a king-size bed would work just fine for Hunter and his date. Hunter wasn't so sure his charm would be enough to win this young lady over; he was willing to wait until she was ready. Hunter looked at the small couch and wondered how he would fit. He shook his head and smiled as he sat down on it and turned on the television. Hunter liked Pieper, and he wanted her to know that he had no intention of rushing her into anything.

Twenty minutes later, Pieper exited the bathroom. She told Hunter it was all his. Hunter got off the couch and headed for the bathroom to take his shower. When he was finished, he went into the bedroom, grabbed a pillow and a blanket, and headed for the couch again. Pieper was stunned.

After about an hour of twisting and turning, trying to get his large muscular frame to fit on that small couch, Pieper came out of the bedroom. She stood there looking at him for a few moments.

Hunter turned to find her standing in the doorway. He smiled. He thought she looked innocent and very appetizing. She was wearing an oversized T-shirt that read: Soul Sistah.

"What's wrong, Pie? Can't you sleep?"

Pieper smiled and tried to hold in her laughter. There was no way that couch was going to hold that man.

Pieper held out her hands to Hunter. "Come on."

"Are you sure?"

"Yes. You said you wouldn't do anything I didn't want you to. I think you are a man of your word. Beside, that bed is big enough for the two of us."

Hunter laughed as he took hold of her tiny hand. "Yeah, I would hate to have them bill me for breaking their couch."

♥

Kamrin let Tuesdae take her shower first. By the time he finished his, he thought for sure she would be fast asleep. But she wasn't, she was waiting for him.

"Is there something wrong, baby?"

"Why?"

"Well, you are usually asleep by the time I get ready to come to bed."

"I thought we could talk for a moment."

Kamrin pulled on his pajama bottoms and climbed in bed next to his woman.

"What do you want to talk about?"

"Us."

"I'm listening."

"You know how we decided to wait until our wedding night to make love?"

"Yes. Well, we never really talked about it. I just thought that's how you wanted it."

"Well, Kam, it's not. I wasn't quite sure how to tell you. Do you know how many nights I laid in your powerful arms and fought off the urge to straddle your strong hips?"

Kamrin's eyes turned smoky as they became clouded with passion.

"You should have told me, baby."

Tuesdae ran her hand possessively over Kamrin's strong chest.

"I'm telling you now."

Kamrin's control was slipping fast.

"I don't have any protection."

"You don't need any. We *are* getting married. I've already told you; I never plan to live without you."

Tuesdae placed her hand over Kamrin's heart before she kissed him.

♥

Linc was on the bed next to Sonja, their bodies not touching. They had been this way for hours. Finally, Linc couldn't take it any longer. He got out of bed and went to the other side to stand in front of her. Sonja wasn't asleep; she was crying silent tears.

"Sonja, I don't like this. We have been together for months now. This is the first time we have been in the same bed together, and I didn't hold you in my arms."

Sonja sat up and wiped at her tears. "Do you think I like this?"

"Love, why are we doing this? Honey, I don't even remember that girl."

"She remembers you."

"Sonja! I don't even know her name. But I can tell you about *our* first conversation. What we did the first time we made love. How good it was, and how from that moment on I couldn't touch another woman."

"I guess I'm just jealous. She's so young. How do you stand to look at me?"

"Stop it, Sonja! There is nothing wrong with you. I love your body. I've told you that before. Baby, you are my woman, and I am your man. That's the way it is always going to be. No one is going to come between us, unless you let them. I hate to say this, but there may be times when this happens again."

"Great."

"Sonja, I'm with you, now. Trust me, I won't ever hurt you again."

"Linc, I'm sorry. From the moment we walked into that club, I saw her watching you. I just knew she was going to start something. After you sent her away, I tried to let it go. Sometimes bad things from my past try to creep up on me, and I expect the worst. Sorry."

"It's okay, baby. You have to understand; I'm not your past. I'm you're your future. Please tell me you trust me."

"I trust you," Sonja said the words with ease, because it wasn't trust she was having an issue with. After seeing Linc's first love, Connie, and now this woman tonight, she wasn't sure how long she could keep a man like Linc.

"Good, now take off that night gown. You know I need to feel your soft skin close to mine. Baby, I don't ever want us to go to sleep upset with one another. If you don't like something, speak up."

Sonja sat up while Linc pulled the gown over her head. Sonja hoped that she had enough faith in herself to believe Linc could want a future with her.

"Baby, I thought I was going to go crazy laying here next you, not able to be with you. I need to go home, love."

Sonja pulled Linc down on top of her nude body and took his hand in hers as she showed him the way home.

Chapter 12

Linc and Sonja had a long ride ahead of them back to Michigan. Kamrin stayed in Chicago with Tuesdae while Hunter and Pieper headed back to Indianapolis. Linc asked Sonja one more time if she was going to be able to make it to the fundraiser. She said she was sorry, but no. Tiffany and Terrell had plans. Her parents had raised their children and were too old to be bogged down with rambunctious boys.

Once Linc and Sonja made it to her house, Linc was not in a good mood. Tiffany and Terrell were at Sonja's house with the boys. Lincoln, Matthew and Jeffrey had been picture perfect. Tiffany and Terrell allowed Sonja and Linc to get her things inside before they had to leave.

Linc and Lincoln were going to spend the night and head back home in the morning. The boys were in the bedroom playing, and Sonja went into the kitchen to make them a snack. As she made her way back to the living room, Linc's cell phone rang.

"Stone here."

Linc's expression became one of seriousness as he sat up straighter in his seat, giving the person on the phone his full attention. As he focused on his phone conversation, it was as if he forgot Sonja was even in the room. His facial features became more somber as he spoke. Seconds later, he was up off the couch and headed for the boys' room.

A few minutes later, Linc and his son emerged from the bedroom. Lincoln was carrying his things. The boy went over to Sonja.

"Sonja, my mom is on the phone. My dad and I have to leave. My grandparents spoke with my mother, and she said they want me to come for a visit."

Lincoln quickly gave Sonja a hug as he headed for the door. Linc was still on the phone when he walked up to Sonja and brushed a hurried kiss on her forehead, and then walked out the door.

♥

Kim had gotten back his report. Much to his surprise, the man with the reporter was a lawyer. Not any lawyer, but Linc Stone's lawyer. What was Linc Stone's lawyer doing spying on him?

Kim decided to make a few phone calls. Check to make sure Connie's son was with her parents. This didn't feel right. He began to wonder if he should have Connie followed.

♥

Lincoln would be with his grandparents for two weeks in sunny Florida. Connie's call had surprised Linc, but he was glad her parents wanted to spend time with Lincoln. They seemed to be please with the fact that Lincoln was with his father.

After Linc put his son on the airplane he went home, he was tired down to the bone. He took a shower and climb into his bed. After some much needed rest, Linc decided to take his free time to catch up on his work. Ever since he got involved with Sonja, he had been neglecting his business. Now he had a few days to play catch up. It wasn't until the next day that he found time to call Sonja. He missed her smile; he missed everything about her.

They talked for an hour. Linc told Sonja he had been catching up on his work, and he would be out of the state for a while. There were some buildings he wanted to look at in Texas. Linc told her she probably wouldn't hear from him for a few days. Sonja was sad to hear that. He informed her that if anything came up and she needed him but couldn't get through by phone, all she had to do was call Hunter.

While in Texas, Linc had gone most of the week without talking to Sonja. He had been busy making deals. He was hit. Linc fought to concentrate; everything made him think of Sonja. He struggled to focus. Linc needed to keep the finances under wraps, keep that bank account huge. Every time he closed his eyes, he saw her face. If Linc didn't know any better, he would think himself in love.

After finalizing his transactions in Texas, Linc was now on his way to Chicago for the fundraiser. He had promised Tuesdae and Kamrin he would make it. That meant it would be another week before he could hold Sonja. Linc's mood was funky.

♥

Connie was out shopping while Kim stayed home with their daughter. Kimberly was playing dress-up with her mother's things. Kim knew Connie wouldn't mind if their daughter played with her clothes and a few of her purses. Kimberly had played with her things on numerous occasions. The girl went into her mother's closet and got another purse and a few more items.

This time the little girl had gone to the back of her mother's closet. The purse she chose had some papers inside. Anxious to start playing, the child placed the papers on the floor next to her mother's bed. She was going to put the papers back when she was done playing with her mother's things.

Kim was headed for Kimberly's room to check on the child, when he passed his bedroom and noticed the mess his daughter had made on the floor. As he bent to pick up the papers, he realized what they were. Crumpling the papers in his hand, Kim became enraged. He couldn't believe what he was holding in his hands. Connie had signed her son over to his father. Didn't he tell her to send that boy to her parents? If Kimberly hadn't wanted to play dress-up, he would have never found out.

♥

Sonja had been trying to get through her days without Linc as best she could. She knew he was busy working. His handsome face kept popping into her mind's eye. Not being with him this weekend was going to drive her crazy, and Sonja knew missing that fundraiser in Chicago had disappointed Linc deeply. She had no other choice.

Sonja and her boys tried to keep busy, but Matthew and Jeffrey missed Linc and Lincoln, too. Sonja was trying her best to stay in a good mood for her boys. Lack of sleep wasn't helping. Sleep at night for her was restless. Usually she could rely on Linc's soothing voice to calm her. The sound of his voice always seemed to soothe her, make it easier for her to drift off. There had been no calls the last few nights. Sonja was feeling so lost without him. She couldn't understand what was happening to her.

Tiffany had said something to her mother that made Sonja stop and think. Tiffany knew her mother better than anyone; they were friends. She had watched her mother mope around for days. Tiffany couldn't take it any longer. She told her mom it was time to think about how she really felt about Linc. Sonja needed to ask herself whether she sulking over him because she missed him, or was she fighting her feelings of love for him?

At first Sonja told Tiffany her words were nonsense, but then she did what her daughter suggested. She really thought about it. That's when she knew; she was in love with him. It had to be love. She'd never experienced these feeling for any other man. Sonja had loved her husband, but it wasn't the same. The way she missed Linc, and how she wanted to share everything with him. He was always on her mind. Then there was the manner in which he made her body tingle.

Knowing how Linc felt about love, Sonja decided she should keep that bit of information to herself.

♥

It had been over two months since Kim's incident at the office with his former secretary. He had placed a call, because he intended to find out what Linc Stone's lawyer was doing snooping around his place of business. The man he hired got right to work.

♥

Linc had been sitting in his hotel room still in a funk. He was trying to get a better attitude, but it wasn't working. He was in a foul mood. He felt as if his heart was hurting. The numerous feelings he endured over the past two weeks were puzzling. Linc didn't like the place his mind kept taking him, to the land of love. He couldn't think about that, not now. No, Linc told himself; he would control those feelings. He was still getting used to being in a relationship…that's all.

♥

Sonja was in the kitchen cooking when her doorbell rang. The last person she was expecting was Nancy. Nancy had gotten a distress call from Hunter and Kamrin. It seemed that Linc was becoming unbearable.

"Nancy? Why are you here?"

"Go pack a bag. You are going to Chicago with Chad and me."

"Nancy, I already told Linc that I wouldn't be able to make it this weekend. I don't have anyone to watch the boys. Tiffany and Terrell have plans."

"I know. I've talked to Tiffany. She and I have found someone to watch your boys."

"Who?"

"Tiffany's friend Rachel. She's home from college for the summer, and Tiffany asked if she wanted to make a few extra dollars. When she heard you had a boyfriend, she jumped at the chance to help you out this weekend."

"Rachel is home? I can't wait to see her. Tiffany and Rachel were like sisters. That little girl spent a lot of time in this house."

"You will have to visit with Rachel later. We have a lot of road to cover. We are going to pick up Chad on our way to Chicago. He heard about the fundraiser and is eager to get there. Chad is looking for a wife. He had his sites set on you, but I had to break it to him gently, that you were Linc's woman."

"Very funny, Nancy. Chad probably doesn't even remember me."

"Believe what you want. t I can tell you that when he heard I was picking you up, the boy almost had a fit. He made me promise to pick him up on our way."

"Does the child know how old I am? And that I have three children?"

Nancy and Sonja shared a laugh.

"Sonja, hurry up and pack a bag. Don't worry about what you will wear to the fund-raiser. I have purchased our dresses, and they will be waiting for us at the hotel."

"Does Linc know I'm coming with you?"

"No, and I can't wait to see the look on his face."

Sonja hurried around the house, getting her things ready. Just before she was finished, Rachel made it to the house and was getting settled in Tiffany's room. The boys were hooking their game up in the living room. Sonja went next door and told Dexter where she was going, and she asked that he keep an eye on Rachel and the boys.

♥

Kamrin was off seeking contributions for Tuesdae. Linc, Hunter and Tuesdae were surrounded by business men and women who were discussing the programs that were going to be laid out for the innercity youth. Tuesdae and Hunter were putting out numbers for them, giving them an idea of what they were shooting for. Tuesdae was thrilled to tell them about the teachers and college students signed up to donate their time to help.

Billie was just one of the young women standing in the group that spied Tuesdae's engagement ring. Billie spoke up.

"So, the rumors are correct! Tuesdae, dear, let us have a better look at your engagement ring!"

Tuesdae blushed as she proudly held out her hand for Billie and everyone to see.

"You must tell me, dear; how did you snag a Stone?" The young woman was eyeing Linc as she spoke.

"Not sure. God just decided to bless me."

The young woman that had attached herself to Hunter began looking at the ring, too. Hunter took a quick look at Linc standing next to him. Hunter was concerned about his friend. As the women gathered around Tuesdae, Hunter leaned in close to his friend and spoke.

"Linc, are you going to get through this?"

"I don't know, man. Everything and everyone is just pissing me off, and I don't know why."

"You know why. Man, it's just a weekend. She is still your woman."

Linc closed his eyes and sought out the vision of her face from the space she had taken in his heart.

"I know, man. I just miss her. Will you listen to me? What has happened to me, man? Sometimes I don't even recognize myself. I miss her bad."

"Why don't you go call her?"

"I don't know. For some reason, I think it will just piss me off more. To hear her voice and not be able to see her, touch her."

"Damn, man. You fell hard and quick."

"Yes, I did, didn't I? But excuse me, I think a certain coffee lady has your boxers in a knot."

"What?"

Before Linc could continue with his questions for Hunter, he felt a young woman pulling at his arm. Apparently, the showing of the ring was over.

"I would like to dance with you, Mr. Stone."

Linc turned to find a very stunning young woman smiling up at him.

"I'm flattered, but no thank you."

Everyone standing around the group became silent for a moment. Maybe Linc didn't recognize the young woman, but everyone else did. Billie Jent just happened to be the daughter of the largest donator for the foundation. Her father was one of the richest men in Chicago. Mr. Jent had not only given a very large sum of money, but he had supplied all of the office equipment. Linc didn't care who she was. Sonja was the only woman he wanted to hold in his arms.

Tuesdae pulled on Linc's arm. Linc gave her a questioning look, and slowly followed her eyes.

"Sonja?" Her name came out in a sensual moan. "Umm, please excuse me for a moment, will you?"

All eyes followed Linc as he made his way towards his woman. There were a lot of disappointed young woman in the building, including Billie Jent.

Nancy saw him first. Then Chad met Linc's uncomfortable stare just before he put a little more distance between him and Linc's woman. That's when Chad noticed Billie.

Linc pulled Sonja into his arms and held her tight.

"Dance with me, baby!"

Before heading towards the dance floor, he leaned in and gave Nancy a quick kiss as he squeezed her hand and told her thank you!

As Linc moved around the dance floor holding onto Sonja with an overprotective grip, he never said a word. Occasionally, he would look deep into her eyes as he pulled her in closer. Linc held her tight through two songs. Once the second song ended, he placed his arm around her waist and led her off the dance floor.

"Are you hungry, honey?"

Sonja looked up into his hypnotic eyes. "A little."

Linc walked her over to an empty table and pulled a chair out for her to sit. He told her not to move. Linc headed over to the buffet table and began to fix Sonja a plate. He told one of the waiters to take a glass of wine over to Sonja. Linc followed soon after with a plate piled high.

"Honey, I can't eat all of this."

"I know, but everything looked good. I wanted you to sample everything."

"Okay, but if I get too fat, you can't leave me."

Linc gave her one of his piercing looks as he leaned in close to kiss her.

"Baby, I'm not going anywhere."

Linc sat down next to Sonja and began feeding her. Linc felt someone tapping him on his shoulder. He turned to give the person a very stern look. It was Hunter.

"I'm sorry, man, but I need you for a few minutes." Hunter looked over at Sonja and bent to give her a kiss on the cheek. "Hey, woman. Boy are we glad you made it. Your man here hasn't been very good company."

Linc couldn't suppress his smile. "Shut up, man. Keep your lips off my woman. Give me a minute; I will be right there."

Hunter laughed as he walked away.

"Baby, I will be back in a few minutes. Don't move."

Linc kissed her sweetly before he left.

A few minutes turned into an hour. Linc kept a watchful eye on Sonja while he talked business. Linc had never been a jealous man, but if one more man approached Sonja, he was going to really show his ugly side.

Just as the thought ran through Linc's mind, another smooth brotha made his way to Sonja's table. Unlike the others, this dude sat down. Linc could feel his blood begin to boil. Sonja wasn't helping any. Damn, she looked good tonight. She wore a clinging black dress, which formed a V down the front, accentuating the fullness of her breast. It embraced her waist. There was an opening down the side that revealed her shapely thighs. The three-inch pumps she wore were fire red. Just thinking about making love to her with those shoes on was making Linc sweat.

The man kept leaning in close as he spoke to Sonja. She kept moving back, but he kept trying to get closer. Linc was just about to make his way over when he noticed Kamrin zooming in.

Kamrin eased up next to Sonja and gave the man sitting across from her his full attention.

"Hey, man; I'm Kamrin Stone." Kamrin picked up an appetizer from Sonja's plate and popped it into his mouth as he smiled at Sonja. "Listen. Let me do you a huge favor. Look over my shoulder. Do you see that man stabbing you with his eyes?"

The guy looked right into Linc's fierce stare.

"Yeah?"

"That's my big brother, Lincoln Stone. I'm sure you've heard of him. This beautiful woman you are trying to come on to, well, this is his woman. You might want to do yourself a favor, get up and slowly walk away."

"Man, I didn't mean any disrespect. We were just talking."

Kamrin gave the man one of his devious, schoolboy grins.

"Like I said, slowly walk away."

The man got up and gave Sonja a brief nod before leaving.

"Hey, girl, you and Tuesdae are causing quite the commotion here tonight." Kamrin leaned over and gave Sonja a kiss on the cheek.

"Thank you, Kamrin. I tried to tell him that Linc would be back any minute, but he just wouldn't listen."

Kamrin took Sonja by the arm and kindly assisted her with getting out of her seat.

"That's okay. He should be glad I made it here before Linc did. I'd better get you over to big brother before he bursts a blood vessel."

The second Kamrin eased Sonja next to Linc, he pulled her close to his side and let out a small sigh of relief. Kamrin took his spot behind Tuesdae and wrapped his arm around her small waist.

When the function was finally over, it was well after one o'clock in the morning. Everyone was clearing the area. Linc had been silent on the way to the room. Sonja was beginning to think she had done something to upset him. Linc used his pass-key to open the door. He stepped back to let Sonja enter first. As she entered, she turned to face him.

"Have I done something wrong?"

Linc didn't speak. He moved slowly to close the distance between them. He pinned her back to the wall and pushed his body close to hers. He had missed her so. Linc was feeling very emotional, and he wasn't sure what would happen if he tried to speak. Frustrated with himself over all the new feelings he had been experiencing since meeting Sonja, he lightly pounded the wall next to Sonja's head with his fist.

"Linc, what's wrong? I thought you wanted me here with you? Do you want me to leave?"

Linc drove his mouth over hers in a hungry kiss as he pushed his body in even closer. Sonja could feel his need for her against her stomach.

Slowly he lifted his mouth from hers, and he pierced her with a powerful gaze.

"Talk to me. Tell me something good, baby."

Sonja's pulse was racing, and she was trying to gather some air. " I've missed you, honey."

"Keep talking." Just the sound of her voice was driving him crazy. Linc began to caress her body as his hands made their way to the back of her dress. He was looking for the zipper.

"I thought you were mad at me."

"Does this feel like anger, baby?" Linc took her mouth again. "Baby, tell me what I need to hear."

Linc was kissing her and running his strong hands all over her body. Her mind was moving like a tornado. The words, make love to me, Linc, formed in her mind, but when they came out...

"I love you, Linc."

Linc stopped what he was doing. He pulled his hard and hungry body away from Sonja. She felt cold and alone.

"What's wrong, Linc?"

Linc walked over to the couch and dropped his large frame down. He was trying to find his voice.

"Go to bed, honey. I will be right in."

Chapter 13

Sonja felt like a fool as she slowly walked into the bedroom. She knew that she had loved Linc from the very beginning, but she had tried to shove those feeling aside. Sonja had convinced herself to just take whatever Linc was offering, not push him.

Linc sat frozen on the couch. She loved him. Did she love him, or was that the passion talking? Would she love him tomorrow? Linc had only said those words to three people his whole life. One was his father, second his little brother, and when he was young and foolish, he said those words to Connie. There was little meaning behind them where Connie was concerned. Linc knew he loved his son, but he had yet to even say the words to Lincoln. Linc loved Sonja, too, but he was afraid to tell her.

Linc Stone had never in his life been afraid of anything or anyone. Growing up the son of Deborah Stone, Linc had to fight a lot. Kids constantly said bad things about his mother, and from time to time, his father. His father taught him never to run. Face it, or run the rest of your life.

What if he tells her that he loves her, too, and she's changed her mind? Maybe he should act like he didn't hear her. It was too late for that, he reasoned. How would she feel if he never responded to it? He did love her.

Linc entered the bedroom to find Sonja half dressed and sitting on bed waiting for him. She looked worried, and she couldn't look Linc in the eye as she spoke.

"I can leave, if you want me to. I think Nancy is staying at this hotel."

Linc didn't speak as he continued to remove his clothes. Standing with nothing on but his passion, Linc remained in front of Sonja and slowly pulled her to her feet. Using unsteady hands, Linc once again found the zipper to Sonja's dress and finally rid her body of it. Sonja started to step out of her shoes when Linc finally spoke.

"No, keep them on."

Sonja almost melted when Linc lowered his head and began feasting on her breast. Swiftly, he pushed her back against the wall, placed his hands under her bottom, and then made his way home in one powerful thrust. Sonja felt a tear escape as passion ran rapid through her entire body.

Linc was full of emotion. He wanted to make sure she knew what she was saying to him, because this was serious. He spoke. "Don't say things you don't mean. I'm not a child that you can play with."

Linc wouldn't look at her, but he continued to go deeper as he feasted on her mouth and then turned his attention back to her soft breast. His mind took him back to that place of whimsical thoughts and desires. No, this was no joking matter, nor was it a fairy tale.

"Linc…" He didn't give her a chance to speak. He pressed in deeper as he captured her mouth with his own and kissed her with such affection that she felt her body convulse as it began to explode from inside.

Linc felt Sonja tighten around him. His voice was shaky as he spoke. "If you meant what you said, then say it again."

Sonja could barely speak. Her body was trembling as tears streamed down her face. Her hands were unsteady, but she managed to bring them to Linc's face. She made him look at her as she spoke. Her words were breathless, but to Linc, very clear.

"Linc Stone, I love you."

Linc moved them to the bed and proceeded to make love to her again. He placed her legs to rest on his shoulders as he kissed the inside of her thighs. Once more, he entered her swiftly with a force that screamed "need." Linc's mind was cloudy as Sonja's love took him to another level. As they once again found completion, Linc collapsed on Sonja's satisfied body while he spoke.

"Baby, I never knew it was possible. I love you so much."

♥

The next morning Linc and Sonja decided to have breakfast in bed. Later that afternoon, they met Hunter, Kamrin and Tuesdae for lunch. Still hanging on to Hunter's arm was that same little honey from the night before. After lunch, they hung out for a while. A few hours later, Linc had to let Sonja go. She was catching a ride back to Michigan with Nancy and Chad. Linc had to stay put; he had a few more meetings to attend and couldn't go back with her. He was cool; his baby loved him.

Hours later, Nancy's driver pulled up to Sonja's house. The boys were in the driveway playing basketball with Dexter and Terrell while Rachel and Tiffany stood on the sidelines with the music blaring as they danced and cheered them on.

Tiffany and Terrell had gotten back from their visit with Terrell's mother. Tiffany knew it was going to be boring, so she didn't dare drag her brothers along with. Matthew and Jeffrey would have had a fit if they had to sit and endure that. Terrell's mother was different, she was a bit over bearing, a control freak. Things had to be done a certain way in her home. And playing games had horsing around was not permitted in her home. Tiffany knew if she had taken her brothers they would have behaved, but she wanted her brother's to be able to have fun, and that wasn't going to happen there.

Chad had been talking about Billie Jent the whole ride to Michigan. That is, until he laid eyes on Sonja's daughter. Nancy noticed it first.

"Chad, she's Sonja's daughter, and she's married."

Disappointment covered his face. For the first time, he focused on Rachel.

Sonja and Nancy laughed at him as they exited the limo. Nancy's driver got out and carried Sonja's bag to the front door before getting back in the car. Nancy was doing the introductions just as the phone rang. Tiffany answered the phone; it was

Linc. Linc talked to her for a few minutes before the phone was handed to the boys. Finally, after they had quizzed him on how Lincoln was doing and when he was coming home, the phone was handed to Sonja. She began to grin as she lightly kissed Chad on the cheek. She then gave Nancy a big hug and said her goodbyes before taking the phone.

"Hi, honey."

"Hey, love, I was missing you and decided to give you a quick call. How was the ride home?"

"Fine. I miss you too."

"Will you say it once more for me?"

Sonja smiled. She knew right away what he wanted to hear, and she was more than willing to oblige him.

"I love you, Linc Stone."

"Now I can make it through the rest of the day. I love you too, honey. I will probably call you back before you go to bed."

"Okay, honey, bye."

♥

Connie was tired; she felt worn out. She had told Kim she was going for her regular check-up at the doctor's office. Connie had made the appointment because she was concerned about the baby. She thought her mood was affecting the baby's health. She still hadn't told him about the pregnancy. Lately her husband had been acting very strange, and he didn't have any desire to touch her. That was fine with Connie. Making love to her husband with the last thing she wanted to do.

♥

Things between Linc and Sonja were going great, but she still had to learn to deal with the phone calls from his ex. Every time his cell phone rang, Sonja's stomach produced a nice size knot. She never asked him who it was, but often wondered if it was Connie calling. Sonja hoped with time that would cease. There time apart seemed to go by quickly. It helped that Linc and Sonja continued to speak every night.

This was a special weekend. Lincoln was back at home. Linc had made plans for Sonja, Tiffany, Terrell, and the boys to drive to Indianapolis. From there they would head to Chicago for the grand opening.

When they finally arrived in Chicago, Linc had reserved three rooms for them. Linc had their first evening all planned out. They were going out to eat, go to a movie, and take the boys to an arcade room. Linc was so happy to have all of the kids together with him and Sonja. He loved each and every one of them. They were his family.

Tomorrow was the big day. Linc and Tuesdae were going to cut the ribbon away from the doors of: The Stone Building. Everything was ready, and it was finally going open. What Tuesdae didn't know was afterwards Linc was going to officially sign the building over to her and Kamrin. A pre-wedding gift.

♥

Tuesdae awoke in Kamrin's strong arms bright and early. She was very excited about the event that would be happening that afternoon. Tuesdae knew once the ribbon was cut, people would begin to pour in. They showered, dressed, and prepared for the days events.

Hours later, the crowd in front of the building was growing larger by the minute. Men, woman and lots of children of various age groups were filling in the area. Tuesdae and a handful of teens were in charge of organizing tours of the building. They escorted groups of people throughout the building, answering any questions they might have.

Kamrin stayed in the background. This was Tuesdae's moment, and he wanted her to be able to enjoy every second of it. He looked on at her with admiration in his eyes. She had worked so hard for this, for the children. He was very proud of her.

Hunter was there alone. He took Linc and the kids for a tour of the entire building. They ended up in the gym. The boys, along with Terrell and Tiffany, went right for the basketballs. Sonja stood on the sideline, watching.

Linc thought Hunter was acting a little strange. "Man, where is your date?"

Hunter waved his friend off. "I didn't want to bring anyone."

"Oh, it's just that I was watching you earlier, and you blew a few young ladies off. I thought it was a little strange, you know, you turning down more than one beautiful woman. Are you okay?"

"Yeah, man, I'm cool. Don't worry about me. I'm just taking a small vacation."

Hunter didn't know what the problem was. He was starting to believe it had something to do with a hot little babe named Pieper Hollow. Maybe that was his problem. He hadn't seen or heard from her in a while. He didn't know where she was. Hunter didn't want to say anything, but he was growing concerned about Pieper. He had been looking for her. The last time he went to the coffee house the owner said she had not come in or called. In fact, she hadn't shown up for work for some time.

Linc looked at his friend with a questioning stare.   Hunter wasn't going to breathe a word to him. He wouldn't spoil this day.

"Linc, man, really, I'm fine. Now go hang out with your family."

"You are family too."

"Yeah, man, I know. But you need to be with them." Hunter pointed towards Sonja and the kids.

Linc looked over at Sonja and their kids and smiled. He gave Hunter a brotherly hug and headed towards the court.

Hunter watched as Linc and his gang laughed and joked around with one another.

Hunter, being an only child, was grateful when he hooked up with Linc and Kamrin. The trio just seemed to hit it off. Hunter knew the same things Linc did for Kamrin, he would do for him. That was the way it was for all three. They took care of one another.

Really, Hunter wasn't fine, but he couldn't tell Linc that. If he had, Linc would have wantd to know what the problem was so he could try and fix it for him. That's just the way Linc was, and Hunter loved that about him. Maybe his problem was simple; perhaps he, too, was looking to turn in his playa's card. Nah!

♥

Kim got his final report from his private investigator. He knew Connie hadn't sent Lincoln to live with her parents. Even though Kim found the custody papers, he still wanted solid proof that Connie had indeed given Lincoln to his father. The report he had gotten from his P.I. was very upsetting to him. Connie had run into Linc Stone's arms for protection from her own husband. There had been several meetings behind his back.

She was painting him out to be the bad guy. How could he be the bad guy when it was he who took in another man's son and tried to raise him? It wasn't Kim's fault the boy was unruly.

Kim thought back to a few weeks earlier. He had learned that Lincoln was in Florida with his grandparents for a visit. So Kim thought he would call Lincoln there, try to shake the kid up a bit. By the end of the conversation, Kim had slammed the phone down; he was furious. Who did that little brat think he was? Apparently, the short time the boy had been with his father had boosted his courage level even higher. Kim could still hear the boy's snotty words.

"If I were you, I would be spending my time finding a good hiding place. Because when my dad gets his hands on you, you are going to wish you never laid eyes on me! My daddy is going to dust your ass!"

Kim was outraged. So, Connie thought she could hide something like that from him? He would just have to teach her a lesson.

♥

The ribbon had been cut, and the speeches were being made. Mr. Jent was just finishing his speech and getting ready to turn the microphone over to Linc.

As Linc stood, he gathered Sonja by the hand. "No, Linc; this is about you."

Linc had told her of his plans, and she thought it was a wonderful idea. But she didn't think he would include her in on it.

"Baby, I love you. Everything I do involves you. Now come on before everyone begins to stare."

Sonja got up and allowed Linc to guide her to the front of the room. Lincoln, Matthew and Jeffrey were waving at Sonja from their seats. She quickly waved and smiled at her three boys.

Linc's voice was deep as it filled the room. "Good evening, everyone! I'm very pleased to see so many people; it's good to know these children have so many who care! Sonja and I would like to take this opportunity to call my brother and his fiancée up."

Linc was still holding onto Sonja's hand, so he used his free hand to motion for Kamrin and Tuesdae to join them. Tuesdae looked at Kamrin, wondering if he knew what was going on. He didn't, but he got out of his seat and took Tuesdae's hand as they made their way to Linc and Sonja.

"Some of you already know, but for those of you who don't, my brother Kamrin and this beautiful woman standing beside him, well they are going to be married!"

The room broke out in applauds as Kamrin pulled Tuesdae in a little closer and quickly kissed her.

"Since I'm the big brother, Sonja and I are going to give them their first pre-wedding gift!"

Hunter made his way up front, carrying the document in hand. As he neared the two couples, his heart, only for a second, felt empty. Hunter forced a smile as he handed the papers over to Linc.

"LB, Tuesdae. Sonja and I are more than happy to hand over to you the deed to this building, and the lot it sits on."

Kamrin was speechless. He grabbed his brother and pulled him in close.

"Linc, man, you didn't have to do this. Thank you! Tuesdae and I will make you proud."

"LB, I'm already proud of you. I love you, man."

After the speeches, everyone began to mingle once more. Hunter remained alone for the duration of the evening.

♥

It was late in the evening, and Kamrin was in Indianapolis visiting his brother. Linc and Kamrin were sitting on the back deck having a few beers. Linc asked his brother how he knew Tuesdae was the one.

"Linc, I've never felt more alive than when I am with her. Even my bad days are good when I can at least talk to her. She listens to me. She's patient with me, understanding, loving, helpful. She can tell me that she loves me without saying a word."

"I feel the same way about Sonja. For the first time in my life, I'm truly in love. What would you say if I told you of my plans to ask her to marry me?"

"I would say that I'm happy you found a woman that could tame your wild ways, and soften your Stone heart! I figured something was up when you broke your own rules and brought her home with you."

"Yeah, but because of my selfishness and fear of giving my heart, I almost lost her."

"But you didn't. You did what Daddy always taught us to do, and what you made me do so many times; you fought for what you wanted. And you won."

Linc smiled at his little brother. "Yes, I did. Didn't I?"

Linc told Kamrin about his plans, how he would get the whole family together so he could pop the question. Kamrin thought it was a great idea. He was just sorry he wouldn't be there when his brother finally popped the question. Tuesdae was coming to Indianapolis for the weekend, and he thought they would hang out at the house, see how sturdy the Jacuzzi was.

Chapter 14

Connie had just come home from her doctor's appointment, where she was told things were going good, but she needed to take it easy. Before leaving for home, she found a payphone in the building where her doctor office was located. Connie placed a quick call in to Linc, because she wanted to speak to her son. For half an hour Connie listened to Lincoln speak about the great time he had with his grandparents, and how much he missed and loved her. The pain in her heart began to ease as she listened to her son speak of the relationship he had found with his father. Connie was happy they had bonded.

As Connie entered the house, she found it to be dark and very quite. Connie made her way inside, moving forward slowly until finally she found the light switch. When she turned the lights on, she found Kim sitting at the top of the stairs. Connie began to walk towards the steps, but bumped into something. It was her luggage.

"Get your things and get out of my house!"

Kim's voice was hard, and his skin color had turned two shades darker.

"Kim? What's going on here? Why are my things packed?"

"Because you are a liar, and I don't want you around me or my daughter any longer. Now get out of my house!"

Connie wasn't sure what was going on. Had Kim found out about Linc, or had he found out she was pregnant and was upset with her because she hadn't told him? She wasn't sure where his level of anger was. She didn't want to push too hard, but she couldn't leave without her daughter.

"I will leave, but not without my daughter."

"You can forget about ever laying eyes on Kimberly."

Connie wasn't going to leave there without her daughter. She started her way up the stairs. Kim jumped up to stop her.

"She's not here, Connie. I sent her someplace where you will never find her."

"I don't believe you, Kim. I'm going to check her room."

Kim started walking backwards towards Kimberly's room, so Connie picked up her pace. She began calling out to he daughter.

"Kimberly, honey, come to mommy."

Connie could hear her daughter calling out to her.

"Mommy, Daddy says I have to stay in my room."

"No, honey, it's okay; come to mommy."

Connie tried to go towards her daughter's door, but Kim grabbed a hold of her arm and pushed her up against the wall, causing her to hit her head on the large mirror that was hanging there. The contact with the mirror made Connie woozy, and her head was bleeding. It was as if she could feel some of the glass pressing into her skull. But she was determined not to let Kim take her daughter from her. She would not leave without her daughter. As Connie tried to regain her balance, Kim rushed towards their daughter's room and snatched the door open. Kim quickly grabbed his daughter up and headed out the room.

Once Kimberly saw her mother, the child began to cry as she tried with all her might to reach out to her.

"Mommy, Mommy. Stop, Daddy, Mommy's head is hurt."

Kim was behaving like a madman as he gave Connie another push while making his way past her. Kimberly was screaming her tiny head off.

"Be quiet Kimberly! You can't go with your mother. Say goodbye to her, because this will be the last time you ever look at her lying face again!"

"Kim, please stop. Don't take my baby away from me...please!"

Kim ignored her crying pleas and continued down the stairs. Connie caught up with him just before he reached the bottom. She tried to grab his arm. Somehow when he yanked his arm free from her grip, it sent Connie falling down the rest of the stairs.

The last thing she remembered hearing was her daughter screaming to her father to go back and check on her mommy.

♥

It wasn't as hard as Linc thought it would be to convince Tiffany and Terrell to come back to Indianapolis with them for the weekend. Once they heard they were going to be put up in a lavish hotel for two days for free, they jumped at the chance.

Their day started out early. Once they checked into the hotel, Linc took everyone out for breakfast. Then it was off to an afternoon movie. Before lunch, they found themselves in bumper cars. Matthew, Jeffrey and Lincoln were running Tiffany and Terrell all over the track. That went on for two hours, and then it was back to the hotel for a swim.

Sonja and Linc watched as the children splashed in the swimming pool. Terrell and Tiffany were giving Matthew, Jeffrey and Lincoln swimming lessons. Linc had made plans to take everyone out to dinner. Once everyone had finished eating, Linc was going ask all the kids what they thought about him and Sonja getting married. Then he was going to propose to Sonja. Linc had the ring with him. He'd been carrying it around for a long time, waiting for the right moment. Tonight was going to be the night.

Linc jumped in the pool with the kids and was picking them up and dropping them in feet first. Sonja couldn't watch. She knew he would never do anything to hurt her kids, but Sonja had always been somewhat over protective of her children. Tiffany called it to her attention on many occasion. She told her mother she should stop smothering the boys. If she didn't, they would be afraid of everything that crossed their path.

Linc looked at the clock; it was almost five, time for them to dry off and change for dinner. He listened to everyone moan and groan, but he wasn't having it.

"Listen, we're going to be here until Sunday, you can come back down later, after we've had dinner. Okay?"

Tiffany and Terrell helped the boys out and led them to their rooms. Linc got out of the pool and pulled Sonja into his arms.

"Linc! You're getting me all wet!"

"Not yet, baby, but I plan on it!"

"Linc!"

"Come on, we need to change. I've got big plans."

♥

Connie had been out for a few moments, but when she came to her head felt as if it were splitting open. Slowly, she pulled to her feet. The movement was making the pain worse. She knew she had to get out of that house before Kim returned. Grabbing her purse, Connie pulled out her car keys and headed for the airport.

Kim drove his daughter around for sometime, trying to give the child time to calm down. The child was in a state of shock. She had just witnessed her father physically assault her mother, and he left her alone, with no one to care for her.

Kimberley finally calmed enough to make her father promise to go back and check on her mother. Once Kim told his daughter he would, she drifted off to sleep. Kim took the still sleeping child to his parents' house. He told them a handful of lies and promised that he and Connie would be back to get the child in a few days.

♥

Kamrin and Tuesdae had just gotten home from picking up their dinner. Tuesdae went into the kitchen to get plates and silverware. They were just about to sit down when they heard a car horn blowing in the driveway.

"Baby, are you expecting anyone?"

Tuesdae looked just as surprised as Kamrin. "No, honey. Who could it be?"

"You stay inside while I go check."

Kamrin gave Tuesdae a soft kiss on the lips before he headed for the front door.

As he opened the door, Kamrin found a man standing on the steps, looking back at the cab that was parked in the driveway.

"Sir, can I help you?"

The man looked worried, almost scared. "She wouldn't let me take her to the hospital. She needs to be in the hospital."

"Who?"

Kamrin made his way down the steps and looked inside the cab.

"Connie, what happened? Who did this to you?" Kamrin raced back in the house, calling out for Tuesdae. She came running, not knowing what to expect.

"Kam, what's wrong?"

"Get my phone, baby, and get the car keys."

The cab driver helped Kamrin place Connie in the back of his SUV.

Kamrin asked the cab driver. "Did she say anything?"

"At the airport, when she first got in the cab, she seemed fine. Then I noticed the trickle of blood by her temple. I told her she should go to a hospital. She begged me to bring her here. The closer we got to your house, the more she began to fade. Then, just as we pulled in the driveway, she passed out."

♥

Sonja was in the adjoining room with the children, helping the boys get dressed when Linc called his son into the other room. Linc was about to bust. He needed to talk to someone; who better than his son? He asked Sonja if she and the group could give him and Lincoln a few minutes.

Sonja and the kids were halfway down the hall when she remembered her purse. It was still in the bathroom. She had forgotten it there when Tiffany was helping her pick out a shade of lip color. Sonja took Tiffany's room key and told the kids she would be right behind them.

Sonja wasn't sure what Linc and his son were talking about, she just knew she didn't want to disturb them. As she entered the other room and headed for the bathroom, she could hear their voices loud and clear. Lincoln was talking to his dad.

"...*of course I want you and Mom to get back together...*"

Sonja quickly grabbed her purse and almost ran out of the room. Is that what this weekend was all about? Linc wanted to give Sonja and her kid's one last hurrah before he let her down nice easy?

Sonja was waiting for the elevator when she noticed Linc and Lincoln headed her way. Linc wore a huge grin on his face. Sonja felt sick. Just as the two made it to Sonja, Linc's cell phone rang.

"Yeah?"

"Linc, man, you need to meet me at the hospital."

"Why? What is it?"

"Man, Connie is here."

"What?"

"Yeah, man, Tuesdae and I brought her to the hospital."

"Hold tight. I will be right there."

Linc hung up the phone and gave Sonja a disturbing look.

"Baby, Lincoln and I have to leave. You still take the kids out to eat. Then come back here and wait for my call."

Before Sonja could say a word, Linc took hold of his son's hand and darted for the stairs, not bothering to wait on the elevator. Sonja stood there frozen. She didn't know what to do.

♥

When Linc and his son arrived at the hospital, Kamrin and Tuesdae were waiting for them. They wanted to prepare them for what they were going to see. Connie hadn't looked good, and now she was in surgery fighting for her life. She had already lost the life of her unborn child.

"Linc, I know what I'm about to say to you is going to be asking for way too much, but try to remain calm."

"LB, I don't have time for games. Tell me what's going on."

Tuesdae guided young Lincoln over to a chair where she held on to him tight. She was trying to give Kamrin time to bring Linc up to speed. Linc was getting worried.

"LB, please talk to me. You are scaring me, man."

"It's Connie; she's hurt bad, man. I'm not sure what's going on, but I'm pretty sure her husband has something to do with it."

Kamrin told Linc about the cab driver and everything the man had told him. Linc found out Connie had lost her baby. He hadn't even known she was with child. Kamrin, while waiting for Linc to arrive, had also called Hunter. He, in turn, called to police in Gary. They were looking for Kim and Kimberly.

Linc held out his arms for his son. He tried to explain to the boy what was going on. Linc promised his son he would make the person responsible pay as the boy allowed his tears to fall.

♥

Sonja got off the elevator. She spotted her group. They were waiting for her with so many questions written on their faces. They had seen Linc and his son make their hasty departure.

Sonja took everyone out to eat. She didn't eat. She was afraid the food would just come back up. After dinner, they went back to the hotel. Sonja told Tiffany that she was going to take the boys and head back home. If Tiffany and Terrell wanted to stay in Indianapolis, she would find them another hotel. Tiffany and Terrell talked Sonja into letting them keep the boys with them at another hotel. Terrell followed Sonja back to Linc's house, where they switched vehicles. Terrell took his car, and Sonja drove the rental home. She would take it back to one of their offices close to home.

♥

Hours had passed, and Linc was wearing the carpet out. He was so worried about

Connie. The doctor had come out and told them to give her a little while to rest before going in to see her. Linc thought about what his plans had been for the evening. He wanted to talk to Sonja. He hoped she and the kids were all right.

They were waiting to hear from Hunter, who was waiting to hear from the Gary Police Department. Kamrin was worried about his brother. He wasn't sure what Linc was going to do when he got his hands on Connie's husband.

The nurse entered the waiting room and told them the doctor was going to allow Connie visitors. She requested they go in one at a time. Linc told his son to go first. He was going to use this time to call Sonja and check on her and the kids. Linc didn't want to leave the building, so he decided he would us a payphone instead of his cell phone. Just as he got up to find a payphone, Hunter walked in with a uniformed officer.

Kamrin told Linc he and Tuesdae were going to go home so he could change his shirt. Connie's blood had gotten on him while moving her into his car. Linc asked Kamrin if he would go by the hotel and check on Sonja and the kids for him. Tell her to hang tight.

As they were making their way out of the waiting room, Tuesdae watched Lincoln make his way to Connie's room. She asked Kamrin if he would mind if she stayed behind and looked after the boy. Kamrin kissed her lightly on the forehead and told her he would return soon.

Kamrin went home first to shower and change. On his way back to the hospital, he stopped by the hotel, only to find out that Sonja and the kids had checked out. The desk clerk told Kamrin he just missed them. He heard Sonja say something about going home.

When Kamrin entered the waiting room at the hospital, the first face he saw was Linc's. Linc wanted to know if Sonja and the kids were okay. Kamrin informed his brother of what the desk clerk told him. Linc sighed, relieved that Sonja was still in town and at his house waiting for him.

Hunter and the uniformed officer, after getting a call, pulled Linc to the side. They explained to Linc that Kim's parents had the child. She was safe. When the Vances heard about Connie, their concern was very clear. They were on their way to Indianapolis with their granddaughter to check on Connie and their grandson.

Hunter had taken the liberty of calling Connie's parents and asking if they could make it to Indianapolis right away. They were on their way.

A few hours went by and the Vances had arrived. Hunter had just left to pick Connie's parents up from the airport. Linc was on his way out of Connie's room when he was met by his son and Connie's in-laws. Linc found them to be very caring people, and he was surprised at how taken they were with his son. Lincoln asked his father if he could stay the night with them. He wanted to be there for his little sister. Linc nodded his approval, but asked if it would be all right if he took his son home to get his overnight bag.

Linc pulled into his driveway. He and Lincoln got out of the car, surprised to find

Terrell's vehicle gone, along with the car he had for Sonja. Neither one spoke of it. They made their way inside. Lincoln headed for his room to get his things. He was surprised to find the bag he had taken to the hotel sitting by the closet door.

Linc made his way to his room. Upon entering, Linc knew something was wrong. His things from the hotel were there, but Sonja's weren't. Linc's heart began to beat wildly inside his chest. Linc headed for his bathroom, only to find Sonja's things missing. What was going on? Moving back to the bed, Linc noticed a piece of paper with his name written on it.

The note read: Linc, I understand why you left, so we don't have to talk about it. The children and I are going home. Goodbye. Sonja

Linc's chest began to hurt as he found it hard to inhale his much needed air. A strange feeling took over. What was that…fear?

Chapter 15

Linc spoke with Connie's parents, along with her in-laws. He wanted to make sure they were all in agreement. Linc was going to become Connie's voice. He would speak for her in court. Everyone felt that was a good idea, even Kim's parents. They were disgusted with their son and his behavior. They offered to pay Hunter's fees.

Linc had been told later on in the week that Kim was in custody at the police station in Gary. The last time he was at that police station for Kamrin, Linc, Kamrin and Hunter made a few friends. Hunter placed a call to one of Gary's finest. He told his friend that Linc needed a favor.

♥

Kim sat in the cell, alone, holding his face inside the palms of his hands. He couldn't understand why his parents hadn't come for him yet. When he placed his one phone call, he got their answering machine. It had been quiet there most of the day. Then there was the sound from the cell door opening. It gave Kim's heart a quick start.

Fear racked his entire body when he noticed the two men being ushered inside. Kim jumped up from his seat.

"You can't put them in here with me."

The officer smiled at Kim. It was a wicked smile.

"Mr. Stone, I will inform you as soon as your lawyer arrives."

Linc gave the man a nod of approval and thanked him just before the door closed tight. Kamrin leaned back against the bars and watched Linc go to work.

Linc paced the small area. He was too angry to acknowledge just how claustrophobic it was. He remained focused on the reason he was there.

"Do I know you?" Linc walked up close to Kim.

"No."

"Something about you seems familiar. Let me get a good look at your hands."

"Are you crazy?"

A loud and demanding voice came out, and Kim thought he felt the room shake.

"Show me your hands!"

Kim made a move to call for the officer, but was stopped by Kamrin's very hard stare. Quickly, Kim pushed his hands out.

"Just what I thought. I've seen this pattern before. It was on my son's face."

Swiftly and effortlessly, Linc bitch slapped Kim across the face.

"Wait…wait a minute; let me explain…" Another slap.

This time Linc's hand paid the other side of Kim's face a visit.

Kim raised his hand to shield his face as he begged Linc to stop.

"Oh come on, hit me back. You were quick to hit a woman and a young boy. Put your muddafuckin' hands on me!"

Kim crawled in his bunk and pressed his back to the wall as he shook his head. Linc walked over to the man, his nostrils were flaring as he spoke.

"Let me explain something to you. Connie may be your wife, but she is the mother of my son. And when you mistreat my son or his mother, well then, you mess with me. Do you understand what I'm saying to you?"

Kim nodded his response, almost afraid to speak as he looked over at Kamrin, who was still leaning against the bars.

"You are very lucky we met in here and not on the streets."

The officer was watching them from his station. He allowed Linc to linger there for a few more minutes. He wanted to make sure Linc got his message across. He had told Linc not to do anything he would have to lock him up for. Linc gave the man his word, and looks like he was going to keep it. The officer was glad Linc's brother was inside with him. He was sure Kamrin would keep Linc from really hurting the man.

Kim was happy to hear the sound of the steel doors being opened, but was stunned to see the officer smiling at Linc and Kamrin.

"You're just going to let him come in here and violate me that way?"

"I'm sorry, Mr. Vance, but I don't know what you are talking about. Come on, you guys; your lawyer is here."

Kamrin gave Kim a devilish grin before leaving. "See you on the streets!"

♥

Tiffany and Terrell talked it over. They had watched Sonja going through the motions for almost a month. Tiffany decided it was time to call Linc and make him tell her what was going on. Before she could place the call, Linc called her. Tiffany asked him to explain to her why her mother had been crying herself to sleep for weeks. Linc told Tiffany he was calling her to see if she could shed some light on things for him. Neither knew what to do.

Linc decided to just go see Sonja. He asked Tiffany if she would make sure he could speak to Sonja alone. That weekend, Tiffany had arrived at her mother's and announced that she was taking her brothers for the night.

Sonja was home alone and just getting out of the bathtub when she heard the doorbell and the loud knock that followed. She grabbed her robe and went to see who was there. As she opened the door, Sonja found a very tired looking Linc leaning against the door frame. He looked as if he hadn't slept in weeks. His voice came out barely above a whisper.

"So does this mean you are through with me; that you don't want me anymore? Why, Sonja, why?"

Linc was holding the note in his hand. Sonja could tell that it had previously been crumpled. He didn't wait to be invited inside. He pushed past Sonja and headed for the couch. Sonja fell into step behind him. It had been almost four weeks since she had seen his handsome face. He hadn't called or tried to see her until now.

Sonja fought back her tears. She wanted desperately to hold him. "Linc, what are you doing here?"

As Linc reached the couch, he dropped his weary body down and locked Sonja in his view.

"You know, Sonja, when LB said you had left the hotel and you were going home, I just assumed you had taken the kids and went back to my place. Man, didn't I feel stupid when Lincoln and I went home to find the place empty. At first I was hurt. For days I wanted to run to you and beg you to come back. Then I got mad! Because I hadn't done anything wrong, not this time. As time went by, LB told me I needed to try and fix this. He said he couldn't stand to see me this way any longer."

Sonja didn't look at him; she couldn't. She softly spoke.

"I had no reason to stay."

"What the hell are you talking about, Sonja? What else can I do to prove that it's only you? And can you please explain to me what this note means."

Linc tossed the note on the seat next to him.

"Just what it says, you and Connie should be together raising your son."

"So, you don't want me? When you said you loved me, that was a lie?"

"No."

"Sonja, I'm too tired for these games. Just tell me you don't love me anymore, and I will leave. If you can't say the words, you might as well get ready, because I don't plan on giving you up without a fight."

"Must we go through this right now, Linc?"

"Baby, I am so tired. You have no idea what I've been going through. I haven't slept in weeks."

If he wanted the truth, then she was going to give it to him. "Linc, I do love you, but I know you've been with Connie. I can't be in a situation like this, not again."

"Is that what this is all about, me helping Connie? Sonja, from the moment we met, my life has never been the same. Never did I think I would meet a woman who would make me leave the game. I fell for you fast and hard. Yeah, at first I tried to fight it, I wanted to run, but the hold you had on me was too strong. Everything about me changed once I made love to you. I decided that having you in my life was more important to me than anything. I turned in my playa's card. I changed my whole lifestyle to be with you. Woman, I'm in love with you, and I don't toss those words around lightly. I'm going to tell you something. This following behind you, chasing you, acting like some punk, it's going to stop. I know you, Sonja. You don't want some weak man latching on to you. That's not the kind of man you want around your children. I'm telling you this now so there won't be any misunderstandings. If I'm going to be the man of the house, I can't let you keep getting away with this silliness.

It stops now."

Linc pulled his body up from the couch and grabbed on to Sonja's arm before he headed for the bedroom. Sonja took in the seriousness of his words as they vibrated throughout her entire body. She understood him, but she felt there was more to it, more to his relationship with his son's mother. She tried to break away from his hold, but failed.

"I'm not stupid, Linc. There is more going on between you and Connie than you are saying. Every time she calls you, you take off running. You discuss her with everyone but me! I know Lincoln wants you and his mother to be together. I heard the two of you at the hotel. Besides, I've seen that picture of you and Connie. The two of you look good together. I've been through this before with my first husband. I knew you were out of my league from the very beginning."

"Sonja, what are you talking about?"

"I saw the picture of the two of you in Lincoln's room. I saw the way you were looking at her. That day at the hotel, I had to go back to the room. I needed to get something from the bathroom. I heard you and your son talking. Lincoln told you he wanted you and his mother to be together. Then she called, and once again, you ran to her!"

Linc was so hurt and angry. His voice was coarse, and his words were coming out louder than he had wanted them to.

"Let me get this straight. Based on a picture I took with my son's mother, for my son, and a few bits and pieces of a conversation I had with Lincoln, you think I brought you and your whole family all the way to Indianapolis so I could leave you at the hotel and run to Connie?"

"Don't try and make me feel stupid! I heard the two of you. And that wasn't the first time you left me to go to her."

"Sonja, Connie is the mother of my child. She is in an abusive relationship. My son is concerned about his mother and little sister. Wait; first let me clear something up. I'm not your ex, so stop comparing me to him. Lincoln wasn't saying that he wanted me and his mother to get back together. I asked him what he thought about you and me getting married."

Sonja's mouth fell open. "What?"

"Be quiet, Sonja, and let me finish. I took you and the kids there so I could ask everyone at once how they would feel about me asking you to become my wife. I was so excited. I just needed to talk to someone about it before dinner that night. Lincoln was telling me that like any other child he would like to have his mother and father together. The part you missed was when he said he thought of you as his second mom, and he would love for all of us to become a family."

"But, you left when she called."

"Yes, I did. It wasn't Connie calling; it was LB. Sonja, Connie was in the hospital.. She was pregnant, but she lost the baby. At first the doctor's thought she was slipping into a comatose state because of her head injury. But now they are concerned about her mental health. Her husband bashed her head into a mirror and then watched her fall down the stairs as he was taking her daughter away from her. Connie's parents have her in a facility where she can recuperate. It's taking her sometime to take in the fact that someone she loved would do this to her. They think she should stay in the hospital until the trial is over. "

Sonja couldn't speak.

"Sonja Davis, I learned at a young age that giving my heart to a woman was the wrong thing to do. In the end, someone always gets hurt. So I became a playa. I've never had feelings like this for any woman before. I knew you were dangerous when I held you in my arms that New Year's Eve. Then I had a taste of you, and damn! When you said you loved me, I knew I couldn't live without you; no matter how hard I tried. Sonja Davis, I'm a better man because of your love. Hell, I even went out and bought you a ring."

Linc tossed the small jewelry box on the table by the bed and began removing his things.

"Love, I couldn't sleep well without you when things were good, and now that you have left me, I can't sleep at all. Please, Sonja, come lay down with me so I get some rest. I can't drive another mile without at least an hours worth of sleep."

"You want to marry me?"

"No more talking, please, baby. I need some sleep."

Sonja stood next to the bed looking at Linc. He had removed all of his clothes and was waiting patiently for her to climb in. Slowly she began to ease in bed, but Linc stopped her.

"No, take off those things. You know we always sleep this way."

Linc sat up and waited for her to take off her things. When she didn't move, he spoke.

"Sonja, take them off or I will rid you of them myself."

At first, she took a small step back, but then Sonja began removing her things. Sonja was still in shock from hearing the words *marry* and *ring*.

Sonja eased into bed next to Linc. "Linc…"

"Shh, I just need to hold you, baby so I can get some sleep."

Linc turned her over and pulled their bodies in close so they were face-to-face, but his eyes were already closed. Before long, all she heard was the sound of his steady but light snore. Sonja closed her eyes and took in the tantalizing smell of his cologne and the firmness of his chest. For almost a month, she laid in that very bed, crying herself to sleep. She just knew that after the first few days when Linc hadn't come for her, he was finished. But he was there with her now. Sonja closed her eyes and joined him.

At first, Linc believed he was dreaming when hours later he woke to the feel of Sonja's soft skin so close to him. He was holding on to her so tight. He was surprised she was able to collect any air. As he looked into her sleeping face, he found no need to worry. She looked content. Linc said a quick prayer.

He eased the cover away from her body as he ran a gentle hand over her middle. He moved to her spot and slowly opened her beautiful brown legs. Linc had dreamed of doing this to her for so long, but he wasn't sure how Sonja would feel about it. Today, Linc was going to brand her his for life.

First, he kissed her inner thighs, which produced a sensual moan from Sonja's throat as she basked in paradise. It was the first flick of his tongue that brought her back to life.

"Linc, what…what…?"

Linc looked up at her with need written all over his face. "Mmm, just what I thought. It's paradise."

"Linc…"

"Please let me do this, baby. I will make it good for you."

Linc could sense her uneasiness, but he slowly went back to work. He allowed his tongue to enter her leisurely a few times. Linc moved his hands under her and eased her hips back and forth as he caressed her with his mouth.

Sonja's mind was hazy, and her lungs were screaming for air just before she forced herself to inhalation. Her breathing became rapid as pleasure began to take over. Sonja had never experienced anything like that before. Linc felt her tense up. He pulled away and spoke to her.

"Baby, relax. I love you, Sonja. You are safe with me. Loosen up and let go. Let your feelings take over."

Linc went back to work. He drove his fingers inside a few times before tasting her again. The sensation of his mouth on her drove chills over her body. This time he didn't have to move Sonja's hips as he stimulated her with one swift movement.

As he plunged in and out of her wetness, tasting her, he could tell she was ready to explode. With a greed that possessed him, he was ready to consume all of it.

Sonja cried out Linc's name just as her river began to flow. She tried to move away from him, but he grabbed her hips and held on as he drank from her cup. Linc hovered over Sonja's quaking body and enjoyed the viewing of her climax. When she finally landed, Linc turned Sonja over and gave her bottom a swift smack.

"Ouch! What was that for?" she asked.

"That was for leaving me," as Linc bent down and kissed her on that very same spot.

"And that is for teaching me to love."

Linc moved back to her petal and gently kissed her again before moving back to face her.

"That is for loving me."

Sonja moaned with need. She could not take it anymore. Eagerly, she tugged at Linc, urging him to come home. Linc covered Sonja's body with his, and plunged inside her, going deeper and deeper.

"Baby, you feel like paradise. You even taste like paradise. Sonja, honey, that's the last time you are going to leave me."

Linc collapsed on top of Sonja after his final thrust. Slowly, she turned him to face her. After their bodies began to calm down, Sonja spoke to Linc in a sinful tone.

"I promise, but didn't you say something about a ring?"

Linc couldn't help it, he had to laugh. "Woman, I just gave you my heart, and all you can think about is your ring!"

"No, that's not all I'm thinking about. I'm also thinking about how happy I am at this very moment."

Linc kissed Sonja before he studied her beautiful face.

"Baby, I can't believe you left me over this."

"What do you mean 'this'?"

"You left me because I've been talking to my son's mother."

"Oh, I see. So, you won't get mad when I tell you I've been in constant contact with my ex-husband?"

Linc sat up in the bed and hovered over Sonja.

"What do you mean you've been in constant contact with him?"

Sonja noticed the way Linc's nostrils flared, and the way his whole facial expression changed.

"So am I to guess that this bothers you?"

"We are talking about something totally different!"

Sonja sat up and met his angry gaze.

"Really? Let's see; you have an ex, I have an ex. What's the difference?"

"But…but you know about Connie."

"No, I don't know anything, except she is Lincoln's mother and the only other woman you've been in a relationship with. I have nothing to worry about, just like you don't."

"Why?" Linc couldn't understand why Sonja wouldn't tell him she had been seeing her ex.

"Why what?"

"Why are you talking to that asshole? The two of you shouldn't have anything to talk about. Matthew is a teenager, and Tiffany is grown. His time for trying to raise them is long gone. Besides, they are my kids now."

"So this bothers you?"

"You damn straight!"

Sonja lay back down. "Humph, I guess you see how I feel, don't you? And for the record, I haven't seen their father in years."

"So you like playing games? You like getting my temper flared?"

Sonja pulled Linc into her arms to hold him close.

"No, honey, I just needed to make you understand. I felt I had a valid reason to leave. No woman wants to sit back and watch while her man spends time with any other woman, even the mother of his child. I am so sorry for leaving the way I did. I just allowed bad memories from my past relationships to confuse me. Once again, I got scared and ran from you. I'm sorry."

"I never thought it would bother you. I'm sorry, baby. You are right, though. Just the thought of another man even talking to you sets me off."

Sonja lightly bit into Linc's bottom lip as she moved her ring finger in front of his face. "I love you, Linc Stone. Now where is my ring?"

Linc leaned over her nude body and retrieved the small box. "I hope you like it. I had LB and Tuesdae's help in picking it out."

When Sonja opened the box, she thought her heart was going to stop. In front of her in that tiny box sat a three-carat princess cut diamond encased in the thickest, most radiant gold band her eyes had ever seen.

"No, no Linc. It's too much. I'm a simple girl from Michigan. I don't deserve something like this."

Linc pulled the ring from the box. With more force than he thought he should have to use, he placed the ring on Sonja's finger.

"Sonja, you are far from simple. You are the woman who taught me about love. If I thought you would let me, I would shower you with diamonds. Baby, you are my world, and I plan on spending the rest of my life taking care of you, giving you the things you deserve. This ring is just the beginning. Well, the SUV was the beginning, but you didn't give me a chance to give it to you."

"What SUV?"

"The one we used when we were at the hotel."

"Linc! You bought me a vehicle?"

"Yes. It's in the driveway. The keys are in my pocket, along with your keys to my house and your credit cards."

Sonja couldn't hold back her tears. "Why do you love me?"

"I have to. It's what keeps me going. Baby, I wouldn't know the meaning of love if it weren't for you."

Chapter 16

Linc and Sonja had just finished making love when Linc's cell phone rang. He could have kicked himself for not switching it to silent. With much frustration, he answered his phone.

"This better be good!"

Hunter began. "Linc, I'm sorry to disturb you, man, but I just got word. We are going to trial in three weeks. I would advise you to move a little quicker and head back to Gary."

"All right, I hear you." Linc ended his call. He gave Sonja a very serious look. "Baby, you love me, right?"

"Linc, what's going on?"

"We need to get married right away. I have to get back to Gary for the trial. Connie has appointed me power of attorney while she is recuperating. That decision had been made before her parents arrived. I was chosen because I am Lincoln's father, but once her parents made it in, Connie's father and I discussed the matters at hand, and we decided that I would focus on this and they would focus on helping their daughter to a speeding recovery. We go before the judge in three weeks, and I plan on making that fool pay. But I don't want to give you another chance to leave me. We will be married before I go back."

"Linc, I promise not to do anything as silly as that again."

Linc gave Sonja a questioning look. "We will be married before I go back. Call the kids and get them over here. We have a lot of planning to do."

Linc and Sonja decided to wait until the next day to call the kids. While lying in bed that night, Linc and Sonja discussed the prospect of Linc adopting her boys. Sonja thought it all sounded great, but she informed Linc that they should speak to the children first. Once the plans were agreed upon, they also put in a call to Hunter, Kamrin and Tuesdae. Linc wasn't going to do this without Kamrin and Hunter by his side.

♥

Linc had Kamrin and Tuesdae help Hunter get things ready. Linc was going to bring Sonja and the gang back with him. They would have an intimate ceremony at City Hall. Hunter would have the marriage license ready, and all the paperwork for the boys' adoptions when Linc arrived home. Linc and Sonja had talked about him adopting Matthew. Linc was concerned that Matthew's biological father would put up a fight. Sonja knew her ex-husband, he hadn't wanted to be a father to Tiffany and

Matthew when he was in their lives so she was certain any paperwork that needed to be signed would be done without hesitation.

The next morning Tiffany, Terrell and the boys walked in the house. Linc and Sonja were sitting on the couch when they came inside. Linc's heart was beating fast from anticipation. Once the boys entered the room and found Linc there, they charged at him. Linc was out of his seat before they took their first step. They were so happy to see him, and he was just as happy. Once the hugs were done, Linc and Sonja sat everyone down and told them of their plans to marry. They were all excited; they couldn't wait. Then Linc told them of his intentions to adopt them. He addressed them individually.

"Tiffany, I know that you are all grown up. One day you and Terrell are going to start your own family. Technically, you are too old for me to adopt, but unofficially, I would like to take over the role as your father. There are still things you might need from a father figure, and I would love it if I could play the part. I only wish I could go back in time so I could've been there for you when you really needed me. But your mother did a great job. You have turned out to be a great person."

Tiffany was in tears. For so many years, she had been happy with her mom being both mother and father to her and Matthew. For Linc to step up, and want to have a place in their lives, was very touching. Those few words Linc had just spoken meant more to her than anything her biological father had ever said to her in her entire life.

Matthew was next. Matthew was more than happy to call Linc, Dad. He was also happy that he would have another brother.

Then it was Jeffrey's turn. Jeffrey sat and listened to Linc talk. He had a look of concern on his handsome face.

"So, Jeffrey, what do you think?"

"I think it would be cool to have you as a father, but…would I have to change my last name? You see, my last name is all I have left of my father, and I don't ever want to forget who I am."

Linc was blown away; so much knowledge in such a small body.

"Son, I could never take the place of your father. I would never insult his memory by trying. If you don't want to change your last name, you don't have to. Maybe you can just add my last name."

"That would be good. I think I would like that."

Linc made a mental note to call Hunter to let him know about Jeffrey's request.

Tiffany spoke, and Terrell stood by her side.

"Linc, I have so many things that I could say right know, but I'm too emotional. You have found the door to my heart, and I am more than happy to let you in. Not since Terrell came into my life have I ever wanted another man, other than my brothers, to hold a special place in my heart. It would give me great pleasure to refer to you as my father."

Tiffany went into Linc's arms and cried. Terrell was standing behind her, rubbing her back, letting her know that he was, as he had always been, there for her.

Two days later Linc, Sonja, Tiffany, Terrell and the boys were in Indianapolis standing inside a room located in the courthouse. They were waiting for Lincoln, Kamrin, Tuesdae and Hunter to join them. Lincoln asked if it would be okay for Kimberley to join them. Linc and Sonja were pleased to have her with them.

After the ceremony, everyone headed for the restaurant where Kamrin had made reservations. Kamrin wasn't happy that Linc and Sonja had to rush their wedding plans because of Kim Vance. Somehow, he would make it up to Linc.

Tiffany and Terrell headed home the next day. Sonja and the boys stayed with Linc and Lincoln for a few more days before they headed back to Michigan. Lincoln joined Kimberly and their grandparents in Gary.

Linc had a lot of things to do in Indianapolis and in Gary, and wouldn't be able to spend much time with them. Linc didn't want them to go, but Sonja promised she would be with him for the trial.

Linc walked the boys out to the car to say goodbye. He hugged them and told them that he loved them and would be happy when they could all be together again. Linc then went back in the house where Sonja was waiting for him.

Linc walked up to her. He was trying to burn every inch of her into his mind.

"Love, I already miss you."

Sonja's first tear fell as she threw herself in her husband's strong arms.

"I love you, Mr. Stone." She took a few moments to cover his face with kisses.

"And I love you, Mrs. Stone. Dream about me, baby. Keep me close to your heart, please."

Linc pulled her in closer and captured her mouth with his own. Sonja felt a connection with her husband that was growing stronger by the minute.

Linc pulled away from her. He couldn't take much more. Grabbing her hand, Linc led Sonja out to the car. After fastening her in and kissing her once more, Linc opened the back door and gave his boys one more hug.

As Sonja pulled out of the driveway, Linc could hear Matthew and Jeffrey calling out to him.

"Bye, Dad; we love you!"

"I love you too." Linc couldn't get his feet to move. He stood in the driveway for a few more minutes, then he willed his legs to move.

♥

Linc was pacing the courthouse floors waiting for Sonja to arrive. He hadn't seen his wife in almost two weeks. It was almost time to go inside the courtroom and Sonja wasn't there yet. Lincoln was sitting with Kamrin and Tuesdae. Kim's parents were already inside. Connie's mother and father were sitting next to Lincoln with Kimberley nestled in her grandfather's lap.

Just as Linc was about to check his watch, Sonja and the crew were headed his way. Linc's heart rate increased as he looked at the rest of his family headed towards him.

Linc struggled to remain focused, but seeing his wife again was doing wicked things to his body.

As Sonja reached her husband, he pulled her in and kissed her deep and long in front of everyone.

"Well hello to you too." Sonja tried to catch her breath.

Linc kissed Tiffany on the cheek, shook Terrell's hand, and gathered up Matthew and Jeffrey at the same time and gave them a big bear hug. Lincoln was up out of his seat and in Sonja's arms.

"Come on; let me introduce you to Lincoln's grandparents."

After Linc had made the introductions, Hunter opened the doors to the courtroom to inform Linc it was just about time. Everyone was getting ready to head inside when Linc felt a tug on his jacket. It was Kimberley. Linc bent down to pick the young girl up.

"What is it, pumpkin?"

"Lincoln's daddy, can I sit with my brother?"

Linc tweaked the little girl's nose. "Of course you can, pumpkin; you are a part of the family too."

Kimberley kissed Linc on the cheek and squirmed until he put her back down. Once her tiny feet hit the floor, she was over by her grandparents, giving them the good news.

Inside the courtroom, Linc joined Hunter at the prosecutors table. Linc still wasn't happy with Connie's decision concerning her husband. Even though their marriage hadn't been what Connie had dreamed of, and Kim wasn't the man he had claimed to be still she didn't want to see him spend time in prison. Linc didn't agree with her, but he had to abide by her wishes.

Just before the judge entered, Kim was ushered inside and taken to the defense table where his court appointed lawyer sat looking over some papers. After Kim took his seat, he turned to look at his parents who were sitting a few rows behind him. For the life of him, he couldn't understand why they hadn't come to see him, and why the family lawyer wasn't sitting next to him.

Right away Kim noticed the look of disapproval that covered both his father and mother's faces. Just as he was turning back around, he located his daughter. What the hell was she doing sitting with those people? Kim's skin began to heat up. He was halfway out of his chair when his lawyer grabbed him by the arm and instructed him to have a seat.

"What the hell is my daughter doing with them? I want her over on this side with my parents."

"Mr. Vance, please remain in your seat. Your daughter looks perfectly fine right where she is."

"I don't want her anywhere near him!"

"All rise for the honorable Judge Abel."

A petite woman made her way to the bench. Judge Marion Abel was in her early sixties and had held her seat on the bench for a great many years. She was small, but only in height. She packed a powerful punch.

Everyone stood as she took her spot behind the large desk. The bailiff spoke again.

"This court is now in session."

Judge Abel began. "I see I'm being honored by the infamous Mr. Merrill. What brings you to my courtroom, sir?"

Hunter stood as he addressed the judge. "Your Honor, it pains me to have to inform you on the matter that has brought me here. Mr. Stone and I are here on behalf of Connie Vance, the defendant's wife. Mrs. Vance is in the hospital in Indianapolis, trying to recuperate from her head trauma and the death of her and Mr. Vance's unborn child."

Kim couldn't believe what he had just heard. Did he say Connie was pregnant?

"Tell me more, Mr. Merrill."

"Yes, Judge. It was our intention to charge Mr. Vance with attempted murder of his unborn child."

Kim's parents gasped. Hearing again how their son had caused Connie to lose their second grand child because of her fall, offered up too much pain.

Kim jumped out of his seat.

"What are you talking about?" Kim turned to face his parents. "I didn't know; I swear."

The judge used her gavel to regain order. "Mr. Vance, it would be in your best interest to take your seat and remain there until otherwise instructed."

She hit her gavel a few more time before moving on. "Mr. Merrill, I have reviewed this case, and I must ask. Is it still your intent to charge the defendant with an attempted murder charge?"

"As much as I would love to do just that, it pains me to say, my client, against mine and Mr. Stone's wishes, has devised a contract she would like Mr. Vance to agree to."

Hunter handed the paperwork to the bailiff, who in turn handed them to the judge. There was also a copy for Kim's attorney. As the judge looked the papers over, so did Kim. The paper stated that Kim would sign divorce papers and give up all of his parental rights. He would not for any reason contact Connie or try to see Kimberley. Kim needed to seek help. Connie would remain a Vance, because it would be her daughter's last name. The papers also read that Kimberley would divide her summers between both sets of grandparents.

"Oh hell no! I don't know what's going on here, but I will never sign this!"

There went that gavel again.

"Mr. Vance, you will be silent or I will have you removed from my courtroom. Now, Mr. Merrill, please continue."

"Mr. Vance, what you have in front of you is a chance of a lifetime. I must tell you, if you turn this offer down, Mr. Stone and I will be forced to move forward with these charges."

Kim looked at his court appointed attorney. Why wasn't this man making any objections? Leaning over the man's shoulder, reading bits and pieces of the document, he watched as his attorney briefly skimmed the papers the bailiff had moments ago placed in front of him.

Kim leaned in close to his attorney's ear and spoke to him briefly. The young man representing Kim listened intensely as if he were hanging onto Kim's every word. Once Kim finished, his attorney gave him a brief nod and then turned to speak to the judge.

"Your Honor, if I my client sign this, he will be left with nothing. Would someone please tell me what this attempted murder thing is all about?"

Hunter spoke. "It seems that your client's wife hadn't gotten a chance to tell him, but she was carrying his second child. Connie was almost five weeks along. The doctors say it was the fall that caused her to miscarry. If your client hadn't left her there alone, the doctors feel that the baby would have lived. If he had just stayed and helped her and gotten her to a hospital, they would have been able to save his child."

Kim whispered in his lawyer's ear again.

"But your Honor, my client didn't know his wife was pregnant."

Hunter couldn't believe what he was hearing. "Your Honor, I think Mr. Vance's attorney should inform him that, in the eyes of the law, it doesn't matter if you know your wife was with child or not. What matters is the manner in which he treated his wife. When you love someone, and decide to make them your partner for life, you don't hit on them and push them around. You don't force them to send their son away because you are jealous of the relationship she has with her son."

Hunter turned an evil eye on Kim. "Sign the papers, Mr. Vance."

Kim was furious. He would be damned if he signed those papers. He shook his head no.

The judge spoke. "Mr. Merrill, are you prepared to go to trial today? Because if these papers aren't signed, that's what we will do."

Kim jumped up and turned toward Lincoln. "This is your fault. I am going to lose everything because of you, you little bastard."

Sonja felt young Lincoln stiffen. The mother in her took over, and she was on her feet before she knew it.

"No, this is your fault! My step-son is not a bastard. He has a mother and a father who love him very much. Lincoln has his sisters and his brothers. And he has me. If you say another ugly thing about my boy, you will have to deal with me. And I promise you this, sir, I hit back!"

Judge Abel tried to suppress her laughter as she banged her gavel. "Mrs. Stone, I presume."

Linc stood with his chest pushed out and his shoulders proudly squared.

"Yes, Your Honor; that's my baby."

Judge Abel nodded her approval before focusing on the defendant's table.

"Attorney for the defendant, are you ready to proceed?"

Just as Kim's attorney prepared to stand, Kim turned to his parents.

"Are you just going to sit there and let them do this to me?"

Mr. and Mrs. Vance turned their faces from their son. They couldn't even bear to look at him. They knew the person Kim turned out to be had a lot to do with the way he was raised…always getting his way; having everything handed to him. When Kim met Connie, they thought he would change. Having responsibilities sometimes does that to a person. Unfortunately, not in this case.

"All right then. If everyone is ready, we will take a short recess and return in one hour."

Kim could feel his heart beating, as if it were trying to push its way out of his chest. What had he done? He finally realized that his actions had caused so much pain, not just the pain he had caused his wife and child, but for himself as well. No longer would he have Connie in his life, but his actions had caused him the loss of his daughter and a child he didn't even know existed. In his next breathe all the anger and fight left his body, Kim knew what he had to do.

Kim spoke in a shallow defeated voice to his attorney. "I will sign."

Kim's attorney stood and told the Judge of his client's decision.

Three Months Later

Connie and Kimberley were in Florida with Connie's parent while she finished recuperating. Lincoln would come for a visit before school began again. For now, Kim was staying true to his word. Connie hadn't heard from him. In fact, no one had. Connie had told Linc she owed him a great debt for all he did for her. Linc informed Connie all he wanted from her in way of payment was to make sure she took care of her daughter and herself.

♥

"I now pronounce you husband and wife." Kamrin was so happy that he had finally meet and married the woman of his dreams, that after he kissed his bride he picked her up and carried her down the aisle.

After taking wedding pictures for an hour, the wedding party entered The Stone Building where the reception was being held. As the bride and groom made their way inside, everyone began to cheer. It was time to toast Kamrin and Tuesdae and for speeches to be made. Linc went first, then Tuesdae's bridesmaid. Hunter went next, Tuesdae's father followed. A few more people spoke, and then it was time to eat.

After the meal, the deejay took the microphone. "It's time for the bride and groom's first dance!"

Instead of heading for the dance floor, Kamrin and Tuesdae made their way towards the deejay. Kamrin took the microphone and placed it close to his and his wife's mouths.

"Is everyone having a good time?" The crowd all agreed. They were having a good time.

"Kamrin and I want to thank each and every one of you for sharing this day with us."

"Yes, we do, but Tuesdae and I have a special request. We need my big brother and his wife up here with us. Linc, Sonja, please join us."

Linc had gone to Sonja's table and was sitting with her and the children. Sonja asked Linc what Kamrin and Tuesdae were up to.

"I don't know, baby, but let's get this over with. I can't wait to get you home."

Linc took Sonja by the hand as they made their way towards Kamrin and Tuesdae. Once they reached them, Kamrin pulled his brother in for a tight hug, and Tuesdae kissed Sonja on the cheek.

"I want everyone to know that my big brother is the best! This wedding; he and his wife did this for Tuesdae and me. Linc is always doing for everyone, but my wife and I decided it was time for someone to do for him. Linc and Sonja didn't have a big wedding; they wanted something small. I can't help feeling that they were cheated."

Linc looked at Hunter, and then at Kamrin before shaking his head in disbelief.

Kamrin turned to see Hunter headed for them. Once again, he carried an envelope. As Hunter made his way to the front, he thought for just a moment he spotted Pieper, standing in the doorway talking to one of the guest. He must have been mistaken. What would Pieper be doing in Chicago?

"Linc, Sonja, Kamrin and I talked it over and decided since the two of you didn't have a large wedding or a honeymoon, we were going to share our honeymoon with you."

"Linc, you and Sonja will be joining me and Tuesdae for a two-week honeymoon in Jamaica!"

Sonja began to scream, and Tuesdae joined in.

"Now, I want you and Sonja to share with us the first dance."

Linc hugged his brother and expressed his love for him before letting him go.

"Linc, do you think Daddy is proud of us?"

"Yes, LB. I think we are doing exactly what he wanted us to do. We both found someone to capture our hearts, love us and keep us happy."

Everyone cheered the two couples on as they made their way to the dance floor.

Hunter stood in the corner, watching everyone dance. A young man walked up to him and handed him a note. Hunter took the note. He asked the young man who gave it to him. He answered, "Some lady, she looked frightened."

Hunter pushed away from the wall.

"Why didn't you give this to me sooner?"

"She said not to disturb you, sorry."

The young man made a hasty exit.

Hunter quickly read the note before heading for the front door. It had been Pieper he noticed earlier; she was looking for him. It was too late, she was long gone. Now what was he going to do? Just then his cell phone began to vibrate. The caller ID read Pie. Hunter's heart began to race.

As Linc glided Sonja around the dance floor, she looked up at her husband. She loved him with all her heart.

"Linc, thank you for coming into my life. You have made it better than any fairytale could possibly be. I love you, Linc Stone."

Linc kissed his wife sweetly. "Thank you, love. If it weren't for you, I would still have a heart of stone."

The End

About the Author

Sylvia Holloman is also the author of "Opening Jerred's Eyes, for to open his eyes would be to capture his heart", is a wife and mother of three. For her, reading is a passion, and a great stress reliever. In reading her books, she wants both men and women to live through her characters, believe in romance, and if only for a time, find love and happiness-again and again!

www.ingramcontent.com/pod-product-compliance
Lightning Source LLC
Chambersburg PA
CBHW071353170626
46811CB00003B/1114